Kendrick hoped that his attraction to Kaycee was mistaken for attentiveness to her presentation.

He couldn't recall a word she'd said. His eyes drank in her beauty with admiration. He liked the way the chocolate-brown dress hugged her womanly curves in all the right places. She was as sexy as she was tasteful.

That was the one thing he noticed about her right away. She had class, unlike other women who tried to hold on to the banner of youth by sporting tattoos and piercings in unmentionable and, in some cases, obvious places. Kaycee carried herself as a woman who commanded respect. She was a lady and the first woman who had managed to capture his attention since his beloved wife had passed away.

He decided that he liked everything about her already. The lilt in her voice and the light in her eyes as she talked about her business displayed her passion for what she did. He thought her rich, hush voice was sexy, and he imagined her whispering words for his ears only....

Books by Lisa Harrison Jackson

Kimani Romance

Finally, You and Me
Can't Stop Loving You

LISA HARRISON JACKSON

developed a passion for writing at the tender age of nine. Since then, she's written many short stories and poems, and has had her works published in newspapers and magazines. Her first novel, *Finally, You and Me*, was published in October 2006 by Kimani Press. In addition to writing novels, Lisa expanded her repertoire to include playwriting and film study. She resides in Atlanta, Georgia, with her husband and two daughters.

Can't Stop LOVING You

LISA HARRISON JACKSON

KIMANI
ROMANCE

 KIMANI PRESS™

ISBN-13: 978-0-373-86019-7
ISBN-10:   0-373-86019-6

CAN'T STOP LOVING YOU

www.kimanipress.com

Printed in U.S.A.

Dear Reader,

I hope you had fun reading Kendrick and Kaycee's story as much as I had writing it. I wanted to write a story about a couple who connected in so many ways and had so much in common, the exception being their age. I believe that love is the essence of all things, and if it is shared between two people, it should be celebrated and not denied.

It is my sincere hope that I succeeded in writing a believable, entertaining and inspirational piece. Thank you so much for your support! Hey, I'd like to hear from you. Write to me at P.O. Box 82903, Conyers, GA 30013, or e-mail me, jacksonluv2write@aim.com.

Until then, let love LIVE!

Lisa

Acknowledgments

I first must acknowledge the most important figure in my life: Father God, you did it again! Thank you for the gift!

Nate Jackson Jr., my leading man, thanks for your endless support and loving me in your special way.

My babies, Chandler and McKinley, you inspire me to be a great example of a woman and mom.

I'd like to especially thank the following: my editor, Glenda Howard; writing buddy, Kim Louise; the Harrison girls, my sisters Cathy Banks, Valerie Ollison, Diana Johnson, Carla Harrison and Gayla Johnson; special friends Joyce Parker, Apostles Melvin and Sharon Milon, and Karen Hypolite; and my first "real" fan Louise, who tracked me down on my first book, *Finally, You and Me,* to offer words of encouragement. Thank you all for believing in me. God bless everyone!

Chapter 1

Kaycee screamed out as she slid across the sidewalk leading to her front door. With one shoe left behind on the walk, she tripped headfirst into the azalea bushes.

How had she slipped? Had anyone seen? Was it the three apple martinis she'd drunk an hour ago? The questions flooded her mind.

The bush's bristly limbs scratched her arms and legs as she pulled herself from its hold. Mortified, she looked around to see if anyone had witnessed her fall. To her relief the neighborhood was as quiet and still as usual.

Kaycee stood upright to examine the damage. She ran her fingers across a scratch on her arm and winced at the scraped flesh and curling skin. Licking her finger, she rubbed the tender spot. She looked as though she had been jumping in a pile of leaves; they clung to her hair and clothes. She even had one in her mouth. Spitting it to the ground, she straightened her skirt and looked back to where it had all started.

She spotted her Manolo Blahnik stiletto on its side resting next to a shadowy object.

"What is that?" she said out loud as she hobbled over to find out.

The porch light provided just the right amount of light for her to see—

"Dog crap!" she cried out as the smell of fresh dog feces floated to her nose.

Her eyes rolled in disgust when she recognized that the dog next door had done it again!

Since she'd moved into the house a month ago, she'd noticed that the dog used her garden to do its business more often than not. The proof was in the little mounds of fly-covered poop scattered on her yard, decorating her sidewalk and, on occasion, appearing on her front steps.

The culprit was the black-and-tan Yorkshire terrier that she'd spotted trotting around the yard and yipping at everything from bees to birds. Its owner never seemed to keep it contained, although it had a collar, not to mention a fenced backyard. After the first week, Kaycee had decided to put an end to the problem, but whenever she attempted to make contact with her faceless neighbors, they weren't there.

She looked at her five-hundred-dollar shoes and sucked her teeth in disgust. She had never worn them until this evening.

Most of her life, she had concealed her feelings when it came to things she had no control over. Her MO was to keep the peace. Be professional, pleasant and polite. A lady. But tonight, all that training was getting tossed out the window.

She thought about how she could have been seriously injured had the azalea bush not broken her fall. To add insult, her brand-new sandals were ruined. Anger slowly rose from deep within.

"Somebody is gonna pay for this!" she shouted, as if making a point, although no one was around to hear it.

She glanced over at the neighbor's house and her mouth fell open in surprise. Through the partially open slats of the blinds at the side window, she could see a faint glow coming from the television set. Finally, someone was home!

Gathering her purse and keys while avoiding another step in the poop, Kaycee unlocked her own huge oak door. Her first thought was to try and calm down, but when she turned on the light in the foyer and got a closer look at the heel of her shoe caked in feces she didn't want to play nice, she wanted to get even.

Without even stopping to take off her other shoe, Kaycee hobbled into the kitchen, and headed straight for the pantry where she kept her old plastic grocery bags. She carried the bag back out to where the waste lay. Kneeling down and putting her hand in the bag, she picked up the poop.

"I got something for you, neighbor!" she said out loud with a mischievous grin. Holding the bag in one hand at arm's length and her shoe in the other, Kaycee marched lopsidedly across the lawn to the house next door.

Now they'd know what it felt like to be crapped on—literally. She would hand over the package and demand a resolution before she reported them to the neighborhood association or filed a complaint with the police.

She pressed and held the doorbell. To her disappointment, the pace of the ring mimicked that of a grandfather clock, producing a set pattern regardless of the caller's urgency. Immediately after the patterned rings concluded, she mashed the button a second time.

Her shoe-covered foot tapped anxiously as she waited for someone to answer. Many choice words swam through her head. *Inconsiderate...rude... foul...pest...dog pound...pellet gun,* yet when the door opened, the words escaped her. A half-clothed man stood before her.

Kaycee's jaw dropped at the vision. Shirtless and handsome, this looked like a man built for holding on to—broad shoulders, defined arms, sculpted chest, firm abs and powerful legs. The only words that came to mind were: *God knew what he was doing when he made this man!*

His strong arms crossed before his expansive chest. "Yes?"

At the sound of his rich baritone voice, her eyes traveled upward to the face of a deliciously handsome man. That face was striking, with chiseled features set in bronze, mysterious dark eyes, broad, yet regal nose and full lush lips. Even his facial hair was perfect: a neat mustache and a patch of hair covering his square chin. He was like a fine wine, aged to perfection, distinguished in every way.

"Uh, yeah," she coughed, wishing that she could disappear into the floor. She could have kicked herself for standing there gawking like a schoolgirl.

Somehow his half-dressed appearance had caught her by surprise killing the energy she had built up moments earlier as she'd contemplated giving him the bag and its contents.

"Is there something I can help you with?" he asked.

Reluctantly she held the bag up. "I think this is yours."

He took the bag and peered inside before making a face. "What the hell?"

"My thought exactly," she interrupted, her anger resurfacing. "*That* was on my front walk just now and I could have hurt myself when I fell after slipping in it." She held the soiled shoe before his face. "These are new shoes that could be ruined. *That* is what I've been finding in my yard and on my sidewalk almost every day since I've moved here and I would like to know what you're going to do to resolve this issue."

He closed the bag and held it out for her to reclaim. "I don't understand what a bag of dog crap has to do with me."

Kaycee ignored his outstretched arm. "The fact that *you* own a dog that seems to think my yard is his personal lavatory has a lot to do with you."

"Wrong dog," he replied flatly. "You said *he,* my dog is a female."

Kaycee's eyes narrowed. "Male, female, what's the difference? I know that it's your dog because I've seen it in your yard and I've seen it in mine, too."

He crossed his arms before him and looked Kaycee up and down.

"Look, miss, I understand how you feel about finding this on your doorstep and I'm sorry that you fell," he began. "But I think you could take some of the blame."

Kaycee's brow furrowed and her head cocked to

the side. She didn't understand how she could have contributed to what just occurred.

"Why do you think I should be blamed for your dog's behavior?"

He pointed to the one shoe she was wearing. "You have to admit that the heel on that shoe is high. It looks very uncomfortable and I'm sure it's even more awkward to walk in. I know they are in fashion these days, but could it be that you fell because you're not used to walking in them?"

Kaycee's mouth dropped open in disbelief. She couldn't believe that he was trying to skirt the issue by blaming her fall on her inability to walk in a pair of high heels. The pair she had on were only three inches high. Back in the day, she'd easily sported four and a half inches. No, she knew how to walk in a pair of high-heeled shoes!

With narrowed eyes, she placed her hands firmly on her hips. "Look, my shoes are not the issue here. Your dog is. I would appreciate it if you would keep her out of my yard or at least clean up behind her. You know there are rules in this subdivision."

"Miss, I know the rules of this subdivision." His tone was just as cold. "And I know that one of them is no disturbing the peace, especially late at night."

His words stung her ears like grinding metal, and she held back the words she wanted to say. Her plans for a resolution folded as the communication impasse got way out of hand.

"Look, all I'm asking you to do is respect my property by keeping your dog out of my yard and we won't have a problem."

When he failed to reply, Kaycee just shook her head.

"Just keep your dog out of my yard—period. If you don't, I won't be held responsible for what happens." With that said she turned on her one heel and stomped away.

"Is that a threat, miss?" he called out behind her into the darkness.

"Take it however you want!" she shouted over her shoulder.

Once inside her house, Kaycee groaned. What a mess! First her shoe—literally—and now who knows what kind of retribution he had in store for her.

Speaking of which, the image of him standing in his doorway made her tremble. She had always been a sucker for handsome men, and this one fit that bill. With brawn and beauty like his, she wondered why she hadn't seen him before. She shook her head to shake the memory of him from her mind. She shouldn't be thinking of any man for that matter. After all, it was only three short months ago that she had ended a four-year relationship, which had turned out to be a life-saving decision. Now she had a new life and a new focus. It was all about her. A man would do nothing but redirect that attention and she wasn't about to let that happen.

Inside her house, Kaycee kicked off the good sandal and unzipped her skirt and slid it down her hips, tossing it across the room. Tonight had been a total disaster, going from bad to worse.

This had been Kaycee's first opportunity to present her business, Soulicious Gourmet Desserts and Event Planning, to a popular restaurateur since graduating from the small-business program.

Everything that could go wrong did. First, she couldn't find the meeting place. The Map Quest directions had dropped her off at a dead end so she'd had to call her contact, which was pretty embarrassing. Then, when she got there, she'd left her brochures, price sheet and catalogs in her car. By the time she got everything situated, the chocolate-covered strawberries that she'd brought for sampling had begun to melt.

Although the look on the owner's face was a mixture of boredom and disgust, Kaycee didn't give up. Like a trooper, she finished her presentation only to get a don't-call-us, we'll-call-you type of response before being shown the door. Afterwards, she'd stopped at a nearby lounge for a drink to forget about the whole night.

Then she'd arrived home only to get into it with her neighbor. Oh, her neighbor! He was handsome.

Bump handsome, the man was *fine!* She wondered how old he was. He looked mature, but she couldn't guess his age.

Turning off the downstairs light, she went to her bedroom and headed directly toward the beveled floor-length mirror. Gazing at her reflection, Kaycee wondered how she looked to him.

Her five-foot-nine build was average for a black woman—well-proportioned and round in all the right places, the way the brothers liked it as she was frequently told. Her breasts were a comfortable size-C cup and rested high.

Stepping closer to the mirror, she ran her fingers through her freshly cut natural curls. The style, with brown and gold highlights, flattered her delicate features: cognac-brown eyes, high cheekbones and a flirty dimpled smile.

She yawned. It had been a long day and she was going to turn in. She slipped an old T-shirt over her head and knelt beside her bed, closing her eyes to say her prayers. God's purpose was for her to be right where she was and she would face the next day with that thought on her mind. Little did she know that her neighbor was part of His plan.

Kendrick remained in the doorway watching Kaycee disappear into the night. It wasn't until he shivered from a cool breeze that he realized he was not wearing a shirt. With a light curse, he closed the door. His first meeting with his new neighbor showed him she was hot in more ways than one!

He glanced at Tiki's empty bed in the corner and shook his head. Tiki was his daughter Bianca's pampered pooch. Bianca had asked if Tiki could stay for a couple of weeks until she could find a home for her after she'd learned that her son was allergic to the dog. A couple of weeks had turned into a couple of months, and now it was turning into one year. Initially he'd thought it was okay because he didn't want to upset his daughter, who was very attached to the dog, but since he'd started up his own business, his time at home with Tiki had become minimal. The boarding kennel was fast becoming a home away from home for her.

He knew that Tiki was the center of the incident that night. He'd had the same problem with the previous tenants. For some reason, Tiki had a special connection with that property. He'd tried everything from putting her in a kennel to spanking her, but it did no good.

When the woman had held up the shoe and told him the cost, he knew he was in trouble. He knew how much women cherished their shoes and how much they despised dog mess. The look on her face told him that had she arrived a couple of hours earlier before he had dropped Tiki off at the groomer, she would have pummeled the poor pooch with her shoe.

His mind strayed back to the dark beauty who had stood so authoritatively at his front door. She looked sexy trying to be tough, although he could see the sweetness pouring through her cold exterior.

He thought her bronze features were too soft to carry off rage. Her hazel eyes had flashed in anger, but had held no real power. In a day of hair weaves and colored contacts, she had the handle on natural beauty. In his opinion, most women couldn't pull off a natural do and he liked her style.

He also liked how the black wrap skirt she was wearing had covered her ample bottom and showed off her long, silky brown legs to perfection. Her legs had looked so soft from where he was standing that he'd wanted to reach out and touch them.

He guessed her to be somewhere in her late twenties to early thirties, which in his book was too young. She was young enough to be his daughter. In fact, Bianca was twenty-five.

Many found it hard to believe that Kendrick was in his late forties because he was in such great shape. He attributed it to diet and exercise and good genes.

Kendrick's vow to live a healthier lifestyle had come when his wife had died prematurely from ovarian cancer almost seven years ago. The running had started the day she'd passed in the hospice. With tears in his eyes, he'd departed her room in shock and walked out of the building. His walking had become a shuffle as he'd wondered how he would go on without her. The realization that she was gone set in, and he began to run as if to run away from the whole scene.

That day he ran for about two hours before he returned to the hospice and collapsed in the waiting room. He found himself getting up the next morning and running, allowing the sweat to mask the tears rolling down his cheeks. When he returned, he was all cried out and that night he was able to sleep. He began to look forward to starting his mornings with a run in order to be so exhausted at night that all he could do was sleep. So far the benefits were in his favor.

With a stretch, Kendrick slipped a white V-neck T-shirt over his rippling muscles. The clothes that he'd been folding moments earlier would have to wait until tomorrow. He hadn't counted on anyone coming over at this hour of the night, and it had completely thrown off his schedule. As a former NFL player, Kendrick was used to everything being in order and in control, and this troubled him: why was he so in awe of the brown-skinned, brown-eyed girl? For the first time since he'd moved back to Atlanta, a woman had caught Kendrick Thompson's attention and it made him very nervous.

Chapter 2

"I'm telling you, Sid, if I catch the hound in my yard again, I'm going to kidnap her and send her off to the sausage factory," Kaycee said between strides as she recalled the scenario of the night before. Although she was vexed, she truly wouldn't make good on her threat; she actually loved dogs.

The pair were doing their once-a-week walk around Kaycee's subdivision. Since Kaycee had left Carrington Financial and moved across town, the two friends had made it a point to spend one full day together at least once a month. Usually, that day consisted of sleepover, shopping, dinner at a nice restaurant and a movie or a visit to a club to hear their favorite jazz band.

The small subdivision with no more than forty homes was laid out in an elongated figure-eight pattern. Kaycee had calculated that five times around equaled five miles. Considering the night she'd had, she was glad to be able to walk off the energy she'd built up.

Sidra waved her hand at Kaycee, totally dismissing her comment. "Forget the dog, I want to hear about your neighbor again. Now, you said he came to the door butt naked?"

"Sidra, focus!" she reprimanded. Only Sidra would tune into one aspect of the story.

"How can I focus when naked men are answering doors in the neighborhood?" She looked around. "This is like some *Desperate Housewives* stuff over here." She said with a laugh. "Maybe I need to get me a crib on Wisteria Lane, too."

Kaycee shook her head with a smile. She had to love the woman she considered a sister. As they rounded the curve leading to her house, Kaycee's heart began to thump wildly in her chest. What if he was home? What if he came outside showing off all of his glory like last night? What if—? In midthought she noticed that his garage door was open. She stumbled but recovered before Sidra noticed. Her friend was busy rambling on about her dating woes and hadn't picked up on anything.

As they neared the house, Kaycee curiously looked over again just as someone exited through the garage. She quickly looked away. As she got closer, she peered up to see a man wearing a short-sleeved plaid shirt, old faded overalls and a brimmed hat, pushing a lawn mower. At first she thought it was the yardman, but to her surprise it was *him.*

It was like night and day. The man she'd seen the night before had been handsome, well-built and downright sexy; this man looked more like a farmer in the getup he was wearing.

Sidra noticed him, as well, and playfully nudged Kaycee in the side. "If that's your naked man, then I'm going to have to take you to get your eyes checked."

Kaycee gently pushed her away. "For one, he's not *my* man, and for two, that *is* him."

Sidra recoiled in disgust. "Eew. He looks like Mr. Green Jeans."

"I know, but that's him," Kaycee said, not believing it herself. "That's the same man."

Just as she ended her words, Kendrick looked up, his eyes immediately resting on Kaycee, who was slightly behind Sidra. A smile curved his mouth and, looking pointedly at her, he called out, "My dog didn't do it."

Sidra nudged Kaycee in the side once more. "What is he talking about?"

"I'll be the judge of that," Kaycee responded to him as they passed by.

"Whoa, why are you off in such a hurry?" he said, grabbing on to the straps of his overalls. The baggy material hid his physique so well that she wondered if she'd seen him right last night. "You gave me a real piece of your mind. I thought I'd made an enemy."

"I don't have enemies unless they try to press me on purpose," she replied.

His face relaxed. "I want you to know that I'm sorry. I will pay for the damage done to your shoe. That doggone Tiki is going to get it."

"Tiki?" Kaycee repeated. "Who is Tiki?"

"My dog. Her name is Tiki."

"Tiki, how cute," Kaycee gushed, momentarily forgetting her animosity toward the dog. Despite the farmer attire, she could see the appeal of the man who had answered the door last night shining through.

"You didn't think so last night," he replied.

Kaycee flushed with embarrassment as she recalled the previous evening's scene in her mind.

"About last night—"

Kendrick cut her short with a wave of his hand. "Don't worry about it. Your feelings were totally justified."

"So where is the little booger anyway?" Kaycee asked, purposely turning her face toward her house to make a point.

Kendrick shook his head, smiling at her obvious gesture.

"At the groomer's."

"You may want to look into obedience school," Kaycee announced. "I think she's been way too pampered."

"There might be some truth to that," he said with a laugh. "She did the same thing to the tenants who lived there before you."

Sidra cleared her throat and grabbed Kaycee by the arm.

"Girl, let's get out of here before he gets into some story," she whispered. At the sight of Kaycee standing there smiling, she rolled her eyes and yanked her down the street.

"Sorry to interrupt this cute little tale but we really have to get going," Sidra said. "We have a busy day ahead of us. You understand, don't you?"

Kendrick's brows raised skeptically, but before he could reply, Sidra already had them well on their way to Kaycee's place.

"Sid, that was so rude," Kaycee chastised her friend as they walked up the driveway.

Sidra waved off Kaycee's comment. "Honey boom, that man wasn't about nothing. Look at him—on second thought, don't," she added with a naughty giggle.

Despite Sidra's insistence, Kaycee looked back to find Kendrick standing there smiling, and she smiled in return.

* * *

"I can't believe that guy was flirting with you," Sidra said as she peered into Kaycee's refrigerator. She scanned the contents before selecting a bottle of water and an apple and closing the door with her hip.

"He was not flirting," Kaycee replied. "He was just being neighborly." She was glad her back was to Sidra because she couldn't say the same about last night. Underneath the farmer getup was a very attractive man, wasn't there?

Sidra rolled her eyes and sank her teeth into the crunchy fruit. "Come on, Kaycee, the man was all cheddar when he saw you."

Kaycee took a seat on a stool at the breakfast bar and began riffling through some papers. "Sid, you know I'm not thinking about dating right now. I just got out of a long-term relationship—"

"Which is why you need to get back into the game before your skills get old," Sidra interrupted.

"What?" Kaycee exclaimed, spinning around with her fists planted firmly on her hips. "I don't need to do anything except focus on me. It's all about Kaycee now."

Sidra shook her head in disagreement. "See, girl-friend, that is where you are wrong. You have to balance your life, Kaycee. Too much work and not enough play can make you a dull girl and I, for one, don't hang with dull folks. I have a guy who would be perfect for you."

With a roll of her eyes, Kaycee marched into the family room and flopped down on the sofa, kicking her feet up on the coffee table. "Sidra, I have way too much on my mind to try and be bothered with some man. I'm trying to secure some contracts, you know, grow my business. Now if any of these men can do that for me, then maybe we can talk."

Sidra nodded her head slowly. "Actually, he might be able to do something."

It wasn't the answer Kaycee wanted to hear, but if it meant getting Sidra off her back then she'd pretend to listen.

"His name is Grant Craddock and he's an engineer," Sidra began.

"Sidra, what is so perfect about that? Paul was an engineer. Someone perfect would be a man who shares *my* interests."

One of the problems that Kaycee and Paul had had was that they could never agree on how to spend their evenings. Paul was a big event attender. He preferred the benefits and balls to the football games and outdoor activities that Kaycee liked. It was almost as if their sexual roles were reversed.

"Did I mention that he sits on the board of the Black Business Network?" Sidra asked with a roll of her neck, hoping to raise the stakes. "Give him a try. Kayce."

Kaycee sighed. "I don't know."

"Grant is good people, plus he's fine as wine. You know I'm your girl," Sidra chided. "Have I ever steered you wrong?"

"Actually you have," Kaycee nodded. "Remember that fiasco with your cousin Rodney?"

Sidra's face dropped and she held up her hands in protest. "Okay, okay, so I didn't know he was gay. He did a good job hiding it from the family."

"Sidra, you said he decorated his house himself and his color scheme was pink and lavender. Now if you ask me, that screams *gay!*"

"Okay, so I made one bad hit."

"Don't forget Brent the biologist," Kaycee brought up another name. "I thought I'd have to move when I caught him sitting in his car outside my apartment after I told him I thought we should just be friends."

"Okay, so I'm not perfect, but Grant is straight and he's not a stalker. He doesn't have kids and he's never been married and he's good-looking."

"I've seen your version of good-looking," Kaycee quipped. "The name *Wayne* comes to mind."

"Oh, like yours is any better," Sidra shot back. "Don't forget the Farmer in the Dell next door."

If Sidra had seen what Kaycee had last night, she would take back her words in a heartbeat. "Give me the number. I'll do it this time, but you got to promise to stop worrying about my love life, okay?"

Sidra gleefully tore a piece of paper from a nearby notepad and jotted down Grant's telephone number.

"So, are you going to call him tomorrow?" she asked, pushing the paper across the table toward Kaycee. "Maybe you could meet him for lunch."

Kaycee shook her head.

"I'm going to stop by that spot, Café Jireh. I won't have time for much else."

Sidra's eyes lit up. "Oh, I heard that place got it going on."

"I did, too. I'm trying to jump on it before someone else gets any ideas. I think it would be a great networking opportunity."

"That's a good idea!" Sidra said with excitement. "But in the meantime, let me know how it goes with Grant."

Chapter 3

The atmosphere at Café Jireh was like a warm hug, embracing Kaycee the minute she entered. She wasn't sure if her feeling of being right at home derived from the distinct aroma of roasted Colombian coffee brewing or from the upbeat tempo of the contemporary jazz tune flowing from the sound system or from the eclectic gathering of people.

Café Jireh was the talk of the town. Although it had been open for six months, the buzz about the café's concept was still making good reviews in local newspapers and was getting talked about in a variety of places from nightclubs and country clubs to church socials. There was a little bit of everyone reflected in the café's welcoming walls.

The owner had definitely taken his mix of clientele into consideration, evident from the carefully selected decor. The building's inside was just as impressive as the outside, with character beyond expectations. Light poured into the room through the stained-glass windows displaying colorful images of coffee cups, casting a myriad of colors across the maple-wood floors.

The chocolate-brown, black and orange coverings of the sofas and chairs in textures of velvet, suede and wood were classy yet cozy, like sipping hot chocolate while wearing your favorite sweater on a brisk fall day.

Kaycee particularly admired the candid black-and-white photos of men, women and children, done in the style of Gordon Parks, hanging strategically around the room on the exposed brick walls. For her, the selling point was the beautiful stone fireplace that tied everything together in a neat package.

Jireh had something for everyone and was a welcome relief for business professionals, college students and artists who had been searching for a reflection of the African-American culture on their own side of town. Finally, somebody had heard the cries of the people for quality in everything—shopping, dining, housing and education.

Kaycee had a sense of belonging when she entered through the doors that afternoon.

"Welcome to Café Jireh," A petite woman with a wide friendly smile greeted in a soft Southern accent. "Is this your first time visiting with us?"

"Yes," Kaycee answered. "I've heard so many good things about it that I just had to check it out for myself."

The woman waved her closer. "Well, don't stand way back there, come on up and let me take your order!"

Kaycee did as she was told and strolled up to the glass case to check out the breakfast pastries. Her smile slowly faded in disappointment at what she found. The plate of cinnamon buns with thick white frosting, the Danish with fruit in the center and some slices of pound cake wrapped in cellophane were all too common in black-owned establishments. Her expectations were higher for a place like Jireh.

Her eyes raised to meet the woman's. "I don't mean any harm, but is this all the desserts you have to offer?"

The greeter, whose name tag identified her as La Jetta, nodded.

Kaycee paused to search for words that wouldn't sound as if she were putting the café down. "I guess what I'm trying to say is that I expected more in way of desserts than cinnamon rolls and Danish. Do you have an in-house provider or do you buy outside?"

La Jetta glanced over her shoulder before leaning

in toward Kaycee. "I've been trying to tell Mr. Rick that he needed to upgrade our dessert menu."

"Who is Mr. Rick?"

"He's the owner," La Jetta replied. She reached under the counter, pulled out a business card, and handed it to Kaycee.

"From day one, he had someone doing the desserts, but things got all messy and he's been buying from one of those wholesale clubs."

Kaycee took the tan card. It was clean and simple with an image of a cup of coffee in the upper left corner and the owner's information engraved in the center. Café Jireh Coffee House and Bistro. K. Thompson, Owner.

She shook her head. "That just won't do."

"We have this for a reason," La Jetta said tapping her nail against the suggestion box on the end of the counter. "If a customer makes a comment, believe me, Mr. Rick will listen. He's a good person and goes out of his way to please his customers."

Kaycee hesitated. Her gut was telling her that this was a move she needed to make. She prayed for the opened door. Could she stand the chance of rejection again? The pain from her last meeting was still fresh. However, she reminded herself about why she was in business. Plenty of business owners experienced rejection, especially the most successful ones. All her working life, things had come easily for her, and now that she was embarking on new territory, she had to trust God and come up with a new game plan.

She extended her hand, "My name is Kaycee Jordan and I have a gourmet-dessert-and-event-planning business. I would really like to meet with—" she paused to look back at the card to recall the owner's name "—Mr. Thompson to talk about how my company can assist him in this area."

La Jetta shook her head. "I don't know. Like I said, Mr. Rick was burned."

"What happened?" Kaycee asked.

"I really can't say, except that it really bothered him to the point that I don't know if he wants to go there again."

Kaycee sighed. "La Jetta, I believe in my product. All I need is a chance to show Mr. Thompson what I can do. I know that once he tries my desserts, he'll be glad he did."

"Really!" La Jetta exclaimed with excitement. "What do you specialize in?"

"Well, nobody has turned down my red velvet cheesecake," Kaycee proudly replied, pulling out the big guns. Red velvet was one of those cakes that could make or break your business. Because they took so long to prepare and required the finest ingredients, bakers often shied away from them. But she had a prize-winning recipe that had been handed down from her great-grandmother.

"I never had red velvet cheesecake, but I love red velvet cake," La Jetta said. "When are you coming back so I can make sure I'm here, too?"

Suddenly the old Kaycee with the Carrington golden tongue disappeared and all of the things that she'd learned in the marketing class offered through the small-business association escaped her. Suddenly, she could not remember how to sell herself, let alone her product. Her frozen state lasted for a brief moment before she remembered the promise that she had made to no longer struggle to be what others thought she should be. That part of her life was in the past. She had come too far not to be herself.

All I need to be is me, she recited in her mind. Her confidence won out and before she knew it, La Jetta was pulling out a calendar.

"Let's see," she began as she flipped through the daily pages. "We have a big shipment coming in tomorrow so that's no good. We'll be doing inventory all day. Why don't you drop in next week? Mr. Rick is usually here by ten."

"It's okay to just drop by?" Kaycee asked. "I don't want to be a bother."

"Please," La Jetta answered. "You'll be fine. Besides, a little surprise every now and then won't hurt anybody."

Kaycee's eyes lit up with excitement! "I will. Tell

me, La Jetta, what is Mr. Thompson's favorite dessert? I thought it would be a nice touch to include a sample of his favorite, as well."

"He would like that," La Jetta said with a laugh. "His favorite cake is coconut."

"Oh, I have a coconut cake that will knock him off his feet," Kaycee said. As she exited the establishment, she thanked God for making the divine connection. La Jetta hadn't needed to tell her as much as she did. A rush of adrenaline waved through Kaycee and her confidence began to build. This time, she was going to take control and get some business.

Chapter 4

The weekend could not have come any sooner, Kaycee thought as she reclined in her garden jet tub. She reserved bathing in her tub for the weekends because then she could lie in there as long as she wanted without interruption.

With a drawn-out sigh, she sank back against the bathroom pillow and closed her eyes just as her cell phone shrilled in the next room.

The ringing phone was nothing more than a distant distraction, and she thought about letting it go, but she remembered the business card she'd given to the young lady at Café Jireh. Although she made it a practice to not cut into her "special" time, she decided to answer the phone for the fear of losing another prospect.

She jumped out of the tub and wrapped a thick terry bath sheet around her body before scurrying into the next room. Just as she snatched up the phone, it stopped ringing.

She hoped it hadn't been Mr. Thompson. She began to scroll frantically through the missed calls when the phone rang for a second time. This time she recognized the Savannah telephone number and answered it.

"Hello, Mom," she sang into the phone. Although she had just talked to her parents the night before, she was excited to hear from them. The Jordans were a close family, and Kaycee was their baby and the only girl. Her parents and four older brothers doted on her.

"Hey, baby, why didn't you answer the phone a few seconds ago?" her mother Katherine asked, her voice echoing through the lines. Kaycee immediately knew that that meant she was on the speakerphone and that her dad was close by. She slipped her earpiece on and headed back to the bathroom.

"I was in the tub," she announced, dropping the towel and stepping back into the inviting warmth of the tub. This time she turned on the jets before sinking back into her former position.

"Hey, baby girl," her father called out in the background.

"Hey, Daddy!"

"Hi, sugar, when are you coming down? You know we still have to plan our fishing trip."

Kaycee sighed. She'd missed their annual father-daughter fishing trip last year because of work, and she didn't want to foul up plans for another one this year. She looked forward to the moments that they spent lounging on the pier, catching and then cleaning fish. Where most women would be squeamish, Kaycee actually found it relaxing. Her relationship with her father was great and she loved spending time with him.

"I'm sorry, Daddy. I've been so busy with the house and the business."

"How is it coming along?" her mother asked.

"Which one?"

"Both," her parents replied in unison.

"I'm almost done with the unpacking, but I think I'm going to do some painting."

"If you need some help, let me know," another male voice cut in.

Kaycee immediately recognized it as being her brother, Kyle. She and Kyle were the closest in age and were often mistaken for twins. He'd grown up being all things to her: protector, confidant and her mouthpiece when she needed it.

"What's up, Kyle?" she called out, happy to hear his voice.

"Nothing much," he said, "How are things going with you?"

"Could be better if you came to visit me."

"I know, I need to get out for real. I just have a lot on my plate right now," he replied, speaking of his position as a college professor at Savannah State where he was working on obtaining his Ph.D. in math.

"You probably need a break. You know what they say about all work and no play."

"No, what do they say?" he challenged. "And watch your mouth because Ma is standing here looking right at me."

Kaycee broke out laughing. "I'm just keeping it real. But seriously, it would be nice having you come out and hang with your sista."

"I might have to take you up on that. I need to get out of Savannah for a minute."

"Could it be because of Tara?" Kaycee asked, referring to his longtime girlfriend. The pair had been dating for almost six years and the whole family was practically on the edge of their seats waiting for Kyle to propose. At first, Kyle's actions bothered Kaycee because she was in the same position with her ex-fiancé Paul. Then she'd come to realize that Kyle and Tara had something that she and Paul were lacking and that was love and respect. Tara supported her man like no other woman she had ever seen outside her own mother, and she admired her for that. Kyle, on the other hand, worshipped the ground Tara walked on. He definitely took care of business when it came to her. They both claimed that they didn't need the ring to prove their love.

"Whatever," he caustically replied. "I don't run from no one."

"Excuse me," Kaycee teased.

"Hey, baby girl, do you still have the hookup with the Falcons?" her father asked.

"I may, did you want me to try to see about getting some tickets this year?"

"That would be nice."

"So how's business coming along?" her mother asked.

"Good," she replied and began to explain her possible lead with Café Jireh.

"That's great, Kaycee," Kyle said.

"We are all so proud of you," Katherine added.

"Thank you," Kaycee replied. "I couldn't have done it without you, Grandma Ursula and Great-Grandma Madelyn and your recipes."

"They would be proud to know that you started a business to carry on the family dream."

"Mom, I'm proud to do it. You know, I was thinking the other day how I come from an amazing family. First Grandma Ursula's skill at baking and Grandpa Art being the first black firefighter to integrate an all-white fire station, and Grandpa James being an inventor, we have such strong history in our family and it makes me so proud."

"Listen to baby girl, sounding like she's all grown up," Kyle teased.

Everyone laughed, including Kaycee.

"Kaycee, we'll let you go," her mother called out. "We were just touching base."

"Thanks, Mom. I'll talk to you all later. Love ya."

Kaycee reflected on her wonderful parents upon ending the call. Russell and Katherine Jordan were a couple who loved each other and their children with such intensity that Kaycee could never think of a time when she had wanted to rebel against them. In addition to Kyle, she was sure that she could say the same about her other brothers, Rusty, Mark and Darren.

When she'd informed them of her breakup with Paul and her decision to leave Carrington to start her own business, they'd showed her so much love and support that she thanked God every day for them. There was nothing anyone could say about any of the Jordans or do to them that wouldn't cause Kaycee to rear up and strike back.

Kaycee was grateful for them and was set on making Soulicious successful to honor those she loved the most.

Chapter 5

The big day had finally arrived. Kaycee stayed up practically all night making sure that all of the cakes and candies turned out perfectly. She took very special care in her selections and decided on coconut cake to impress Mr. Thompson's taste buds and her famous red velvet cheesecake to win over La Jetta, as well as German chocolate cake, Italian cream cake and fresh peach cobbler. On top of that, she had made some chocolate-covered strawberries and truffles. Each dessert was neatly packaged in custom-made turquoise-blue-and-chocolate-brown boxes and tied with a shiny gold ribbon displaying the company name.

This time she was not going to get caught with cake on her face as she'd done the other night. Just remembering her failed meeting made her triple-check to ensure that everything was in order. Before she went to bed, she stocked her briefcase with the high-gloss, full-color catalog, order forms and business cards and placed it in the trunk of her car. She also took the time to make sure that her appearance spoke of class and professionalism. To keep with the color scheme, she chose to wear her chocolate-brown wrap dress with a turquoise-and-brown scarf tied around her neck and a pair of matching brown sandals.

For a change of pace, she worked some styling mousse into her hair, forming curly ringlets that framed her face. She smiled with satisfaction at the completed reflection in the mirror. After she loaded the car, she paused at the door to say a short prayer.

"Father God, I thank you for being the lord over my life. Thank you for ordering my steps. Lord, you told me that I can do all things through Christ who strengthens me. I believe that today you are opening up a door for me and I thank you in advance. Give me wisdom, oh Lord, to say the right things. Help me not to forget anything. Thank you for Your favor, in Jesus' name, amen."

The ride to the café was a mere ten minutes, which was enough time for her to think. She thought about the business and how she was fulfilling her destiny. In less than a year, her life had taken a dramatic turn. First, she had left her job to pursue her business dream and then she had left Paul.

Her job had been monetarily rewarding but was so stressful that it left her drained at the end of the day. Her midtown condo was located in a very desirable neighborhood within walking distance of all the "hot" spots of dining and night life, but it wasn't something she enjoyed any longer.

Then there was her boyfriend Paul: she was practically on pins and needles waiting for him to propose, yet every birthday, Christmas and Valentine's Day passed without a word about the prospect of marriage. By the time last Christmas had rolled around, Kaycee had grown lukewarm to the idea of marriage, at least to Paul. So, when he got down on one knee during a jazz concert and proposed, she was tongue-tied. She could not say or do anything but shake her head no. It was at that precise moment that she knew the facade that she called her life was coming to an end and the real Kaycee Janae Jordan was coming to life.

Words of disappointment were expressed and tears shed when Kaycee admitted that she didn't have the heart to go on with their relationship. She spent most of that night evaluating her life and realized that there were many things that she didn't like but had given into because they had been expected of her.

Paul Copeland, for example, had stepped into Kaycee's personal space at a business event with a seductive smile, making her flush with flattery from his attention. Kaycee had told him that she was a recent MBA graduate looking for a job, and attended the event in the hopes of getting some leads. Without a word, Paul immediately took her by the hand, led her across the room and introduced her to Gina Stall-worth, who would become her future boss. A week later, she was at Carrington Financial Group.

Gradually, Kaycee found her appearance changing. Her hair was one of the first transformations. It was thick and coarse and came only to her ears so Paul suggested weaves. Although the long-layered style looked good and complemented her beautiful eyes, she hated finding stray hairs all over the house, especially in the shower drain and in corners on the bathroom floor.

Natural styles were frowned upon in the Carrington environment, especially for management. Her desire to emancipate came while she was out at lunch with other managers. The group was rattling on about a client. Kaycee was there in body, but she had abandoned them in spirit by choosing to focus her attention on their surroundings. Then it happened. A beautiful black woman entered the restaurant. She seemed the embodiment of poise and power as she strolled past as if walking on a catwalk in a fashion show. The fitted T-shirt, flare-legged jeans and big curly Afro spoke volumes to Kaycee. This was a proud sista' who wasn't stepping aside to measure up to the world's expectations, but who was demanding that the world step up to meet hers. After she paid for her takeout, she passed their table she smiled at Kaycee with a slight nod, and it was like confirmation that change would have to come. Downsizing quickly became a major focus in all areas of her life. She got rid of the man, quit her job, moved to the suburbs, took out her weaves and donated much of her pricey wardrobe to a welfare-to-work program. Now she was exactly where she wanted to be in life and she couldn't be happier.

Café Jireh was located in the growing section of midtown Atlanta called Atlantic Station, a popular live, work and play community made up of hotels, upscale boutiques and fine restaurants merged with expensive condos.

Kaycee was relieved to find an available parking space right out front. A quick glance at her watch told her that she was ten minutes ahead of schedule, so she had time to relax and focus on her presentation, however, her nerves got the best of her and she gave in to them and went inside.

The moment she entered, Kaycee grew nervous at the sight of a different face at the counter. She had been counting on La Jetta's easygoing friendliness as support and confirmation to ease her fears. The woman standing behind the counter looked nice enough, but didn't immediately generate the same kind of outgoing attitude that she had encountered with La Jetta. She was older with graying hair smoothed into a neat bun and glasses on the tip of her nose.

"Good morning," Kaycee greeted with her warmest smile. "I have an appointment with Mr. Thompson."

The woman slowly shook her head and peered sternly at Kaycee over the rims of her glasses. "Mr. Rick don't meet with nobody on Mondays."

Kaycee's mouth grew dry and she swallowed hard. "I talked to La Jetta last week and she said this would be a good time to meet with Mr. Thompson."

The older woman shook her head with a drawn-out sigh as if she had heard that excuse before. "I don't know why Jetta acts like she's trying to be Mr. Rick's secretary. She knows better than that." She looked down at the basket in Kaycee's hands. "What kind of meeting do you have?"

Kaycee placed the basket on the counter and took out a business card. She handed it to the woman.

"My name is Kaycee Jordan and I was talking to La Jetta about doing business with Mr. Thompson."

The woman sucked her teeth and shook her head. "Jetta know Mr. Rick said he wasn't trying to get anyone else to fill that position."

"May I ask why?" Kaycee asked. La Jetta's explanation had been a little sketchy, and she wanted to know what she was dealing with.

"He was burned," she replied. "That's all I can say."

"I'm sorry to hear that," Kaycee answered. Then a thought came to her. She was going to get to Mr. Rick today by any means necessary. She reached inside the basket and took out a container of peach cobbler.

"I know what it's like to have trust in someone and have them fail you," Kaycee said removing the lid from the box to retrieve the small container inside. She placed the container in front of the woman and allowed the sweet smell of peaches, cinnamon and buttery crust to entice her nose.

"Wh-what's that?" the older woman stammered, her eyes lighting up at the gift before her.

"My grandmother Ursula's peach cobbler recipe," Kaycee replied. "I'm told that one taste and you'll never go back to instant cobbler again."

"Is that right?" she said, smacking her lips. Her eyes were big as saucers and Kaycee swore she could see saliva building up in the corners of her mouth.

"Why not try for yourself?" She handed her a clear plastic spoon.

The woman scooped some of the dessert in the spoon and examined it closely. She took a whiff and nodded as if the filling and crust were the right consistency. She brought the spoon to her face and eyed it for a few seconds more before placing it into her mouth.

Kaycee watched her face intently, but she just continued to chomp away as if she had no opinion one way or the other. She finally looked up at Kaycee after finishing her bite. Her eyes traveled back to the basket.

"What else you got in there?"

Kaycee's heartbeat quickened and she scrambled to open the basket to reveal its contents. "I have coconut cake, German chocolate cake, Italian cream cake and red velvet cheesecake plus some chocolate-covered strawberries and truffles."

"Wait right here," the woman said and disappeared to the back.

The minutes seemed like hours to Kaycee, and she prayed that her strawberries and truffles were still holding up. She sighed with relief when the lady returned. She seemed like a different person.

"Go on and have a seat over at the table there, sugah, and Mr. Rick will be out with you shortly."

"Thank you," Kaycee whispered with a sigh of relief. "Thank you very much." She quickly gathered her things and went to set up the table that the woman had pointed out. First she laid out a turquoise satin tablecloth. Then she removed the boxes containing the goodies. To her relief each one was intact. She removed the lids and propped the boxes atop them around the table. Before one chair she placed a gold fork, a china plate and one of the colorful catalogs with an order form and business card.

With a satisfied grin, she sat back and waited. Customers threw curious glances her way wondering what the occasion was. A few even stopped to admire her wares and take business cards.

The woman came over to the table to praise her for her creativity and offered her a cup of coffee on the house.

"What do you recommend?"

"All of it, but I'll give you the toffee crunch," she answered. Before she walked away she turned back and smiled again, saying, "By the way, my name is Charlotte and I think your peach cobbler is delicious!"

Kaycee smiled proudly. "Thank you so much."

She looked back to the table and straightened the papers across from her once more. Suddenly, she felt a presence. Slowly looking up, her breath caught at the sight of her neighbor standing before her.

Chapter 6

The last person she wanted to see was him. He was too much of a distraction and concentration was important for this meeting. However, she could not deny how fine he looked in the pale yellow dress shirt and black tailored trousers, compared to the overalls and plaid shirt he'd had on a few days ago. The man was like a chameleon. Whatever he was there for, she hoped he'd get it and be well on his way.

"What are you doing here?" she whispered.

"My question exactly," he replied.

"For your information, I'm here for an important

business meeting, so I don't have time to get into it with you over your dog."

Kendrick's face fell. "Don't tell me that you're Kaycee Jordan from Soulicious?"

"Why?" The look on his face told it all. He was Kendrick Thompson. "You can't be," she stuttered.

"I am," he replied. His eyes took in the spread on the table before her. "What is all of this?" he asked with a wave of his arm.

"It's a part of my presentation."

"Do you think all of that is necessary?" His tone reminded her of the flippant comment about her shoes and she immediately went on the defensive.

"For my business it is," she carefully replied. "I happen to take what I do very seriously and I treat all of my clients with the utmost professionalism. So if you'd care to hear my presentation, I would like to get on with it."

A slow smile curved Kendrick's lips and he nodded for her to proceed. He pulled out the bistro chair and took a seat.

Kendrick hoped that his attraction to Kaycee would be mistaken for attentiveness to her presentation. If asked, he probably couldn't recall a word she said. His eyes drank in her beauty. He liked the way the choclate-brown dress hugged her womanly curves in all the right places. Although sexy, it was tasteful.

That was the one thing he noticed about her right away. She had class, unlike other women who tried to hold on to the banner of youth by sporting tattoos and piercings in unmentionable and in some cases obvious places, Kaycee carried herself as a woman who commanded respect. She was the first woman who had managed to capture his attention since his beloved wife had passed away.

He decided that he liked everything about her already. The lilt in her voice and the light in her eyes as she talked about her business displayed her passion for what she did. He thought her rich, husky voice was sexy and he imagined her whispering words for his ears only.

"Mr. Thompson, I said would you like to sample some of the cake?" she repeated in a soft voice as smooth as a caress.

Kendrick jumped out of his daydream and cleared his throat nervously. "Huh, wh-what?" He looked up to find her standing over him with a gold fork and a plate in hand.

"Cake," she said holding out the plate. "Would you like some?"

"Sure," he replied. He couldn't deny that his attention had zeroed in on the coconut cake when he'd first arrived at the table. Charlotte had raved over the peach cobbler. If the coconut cake was as good, he might have to consider doing business with Kaycee.

Kaycee transferred the cake from the box onto the plate and placed it before him.

Kendrick took the fork and dug in. The taste reminded him of Sunday afternoons when he and his brothers and sisters had looked forward to their mother's coconut cake after church. Kaycee's was just as moist and just as delicious.

"This is good," he announced.

Kaycee's eyes widened at the look of passion in Kendrick's face as he ate. She had never seen a man show so much expression. The way his full lips savored the cake made her want to jump on the plate, too. The whole experience was almost…orgasmic!

"Try some of the Italian cream cake and tell me what you think." She slid a corner of the cake onto his plate. The second the cake hit his mouth, it seemed to melt.

"Mmm, mmm, mmm," he moaned. "Are you sure that you made these?"

"What are you trying to imply?" she asked, surprised by another one of his offhand comments.

Kendrick shrugged and wiped his mouth on the napkin she provided. "It's just that you're kind of young, and I thought people your age would be more interested in buying a cake than baking one."

Her first reaction was to cut him off with a sharp comment, but what would that accomplish? Nothing.

Would it get her the business she was trying to secure? Probably not. So she chose to take the high road.

"Mr. Thompson, understand this. I'm a very serious business woman. Baking is now my life. Every one of these recipes has been handed down from generations. I'm offended that you'd think I would try to accomplish something by taking short-cuts. That's not my style."

Kendrick reared his head back to look her squarely in the eye. "I'm sorry. Please forgive me for my lack of professionalism. It's just that I've been in this situation before. I know you don't have anything to do with it, but it's kind of hard getting over."

She exhaled slowly, relieved that he wasn't the monster she thought him to be. "I'll accept your apology if you place an order."

"And if I don't?"

Kaycee paused and looked into his eyes and struggled for a witty comeback, but she had none to throw. With a sigh she just shook her head in defeat. The man was definitely a challenge.

The silence was comforting yet awkward at the same time. Kendrick tilted his head to the side and his eyes lowered as if studying the depths of her soul, just as they had the other night. Kaycee squirmed under his gaze, but she couldn't look away. He had her locked in.

He's doing it again, she thought. He's giving me that same look that makes me…

"I have an event coming up sponsored by the Soul Connection—ever hear of them?"

Kaycee's eyes widened in recognition of the popular local dating club. It was full of well-to-do young professionals with lots of connections. She nodded.

"Your product is perfect. I may consider working with you. Why don't you leave these with me," he said, picking up one of her catalogs and an order form. "I'll call you later in the week to let you know where I stand. Fair enough?"

"Fair enough," she replied, placing her hand into his. As their hands touched, Kaycee sucked in a breath at the current of energy that transferred between them. She didn't know what Kendrick Thompson was all about, but she had a distinct feeling that she would soon find out.

Chapter 7

Kendrick found it difficult to focus on the papers before him. He had his work cut out for him. In exactly one week, Café Jireh would be alive with singles hoping to make a love connection. Kendrick had been honored when the president of Soul Connection called to request a large party reservation.

To impress the attendees, Kendrick wanted to go all-out. He'd thought about hiring a band, clearing a space for a dance floor and planning a special dinner and dessert buffet.

Everything had to go off without incident. So he called in the big guns, Martinique Rivers of Finest

Affairs Special Event Planning Team, who also happened to be one of his former lovers.

He didn't really want to have Martinique plan the event but she was one of the city's most talented event planners. When they'd parted a year ago, Kendrick had known it was for the best. Martinique had wanted something from him that he wasn't ready to give—at least to her. But since the café had taken off, he'd quickly realized that his hands were full, and he needed to recruit someone who could put on an excellent affair for an excellent price and he knew he could get both from Martinique.

"Mr. Rick," a voice called out, interrupting his thoughts.

Kendrick glanced up to find Charlotte wearing a bothered expression.

"Charlotte, what's wrong?"

The older woman rolled her eyes and through tight lips announced, "Ms. Rivers is here to see you."

His eyes rolled back in his head and he sighed deeply. "Tell her that I'll be out in a second."

Instead of doing what she was told, Charlotte stepped inside the small office and closed the door.

"Mr. Rick, why is she here?" she whispered. "I thought you said it was over between you two."

Kendrick ran his palm over his head and sighed. "Charlotte, it is over, but I need her help."

"In what way?" the older lady snapped. "She

helped you last time when she almost cost you your
business. You remember that, don't ya? Why you
foolin' with her again?"

He stood up behind his desk. "Charlotte. I have
the Soul Connection affair coming up next week
and I don't have one thing planned. Martinique is
good at that."

He was ashamed to admit that he didn't have any
plans. Each time he tried to sit down to generate
ideas he was pulled in another direction. Last week
it had been his daughter Bianca. She'd been working
late in court and needed Kendrick to pick up his two-
year-old grandson, Sebastian, from daycare. This
week it was Kaycee.

Since their run-in, followed by the meeting a few
days ago, Kendrick could not get her off his mind.
From the time he rose each morning until he left the
house, his thoughts were on her. Each morning, he
hoped to catch a glimpse of her walking the neighborhood or leaving her house, but their paths never
crossed. When he returned late in the evenings, he
found himself glancing at her house to see if there
was life, but it was always quiet.

Since the latest incident with Tiki, he'd been extra
careful about letting the dog roam so freely. He must
have been doing a better job than he thought, because
he hadn't heard a single complaint.

He thought about how Kaycee's business would

be a welcome addition to the café. He knew he needed delicious desserts to complement the coffees, and Kaycee's fare fit the bill, but he was having a hard time making up his mind. He had been burned and he wasn't ready to go there yet.

Her name was Antoinette. She'd breezed into Kendrick's life shortly after he'd moved back to the Atlanta area. They'd met at an art gallery. She was a recent divorcée with a teenage son, a gorgeous face and beautiful body.

Right away, she had let him know that she found him attractive, too, and wanted to see him on a personal level. Although he'd told her that he wasn't looking for a relationship, she'd pursued him anyway. At first their relationship was strictly platonic.

They hung out, caught a movie here and there, attended plays and jazz concerts in the park. They also shared a passion for business. It was common to find them at the local diner hashing out business ideas.

Kendrick had told Antoinette about his desire to open the café and she'd insisted that she wanted to help. In turn, Antoinette connected him with the people he needed to make the paperwork move faster. She'd also enlisted her uncle who was a pastry chef at a famous L.A. restaurant to ship desserts. Everything appeared to be on the up and up and Kendrick began entertaining the idea of opening up his heart again. So he'd let down his defenses and began to initiate dates. He and Antoinette enjoyed his favorite pastimes like picnics in the park, riding his motorcycle and fishing—but it wasn't enough.

Right before he was to open the doors to Café Jireh, Antoinette handed him a contract stating that she would be a silent partner and would reap forty-five percent of all earnings from the restaurant. Attached to it was a list of those tasks that she had so "graciously" performed for him.

Kendrick was taken by surprise and he quietly paid her out of the picture, vowing to keep his personal and business lives separate, which is why he didn't want to move forward with Kaycee. He was attracted to her, and to the fact that she had an excellent product, but he couldn't bare to repeat the Antoinette fiasco.

"Mr. Rick, Mr. Rick," Charlotte called while snapping her fingers before his face.

"I'm sorry, Charlotte," he apologized. "I guess I was daydreaming."

"I said, what do you want me to tell old starch britches out there?" she asked, nudging her head toward the dining room.

Kendrick chuckled. Martinique had a reputation around Jireh as the ice queen who surreptitiously hid her royal scepter up her behind.

He stood up with the party file in hand and draped

his arm across Charlotte's shoulders. "Don't worry, I'll take it from here."

Kendrick spotted Martinique sitting in a corner booth, tapping away on her laptop while holding a conversation on her cell phone, as usual.

With a deep sigh he approached, hoping that he wasn't making a mistake.

She looked up as he got nearer. "Kendrick, darling!" she said, standing up; her three-inch heels placed her eye to eye with him. She had an aristocratic air about her and a blue-blood pedigree to match. She frequently bragged about how she could trace her generations back to one of the oldest, most prominent African-American families in Atlanta.

They exchanged air kisses.

"Martinique, thank you for coming," he said and waited for her to sit down before taking a chair across from her.

Martinique reclaimed her seat and signed off from her call. She placed the cell phone on the table and took Kendrick's hand in hers. "Ken, you know I'm honored that you would ask me to help you."

"I couldn't think of anyone else who'd be better for the job." He failed to mention that his main purpose for calling was so that he could assign all of the coordinating to her. He neither had the time nor did he have the energy to do it with business as busy as it was. Besides, he knew that with her connections, she could put on an affair that would keep people talking about Jireh.

Martinique giggled. "Now, tell me the good stuff. Are you interested in something safe and affordable—a Honda party—or are you looking for something elite and memorable—a Bentley party?"

Kendrick shook his head with a laugh at her analogy. Martinique was something else. As he leaned forward to explain what he wanted, he didn't notice the pearl-white Toyota pulling up outside and Kaycee stepping out.

"Hi, Charlotte, how are you?" Kaycee greeted the woman behind the counter with a smile.

Charlotte's face lit up with joy. "Ms. Jordan, how are you?"

"Kaycee, please call me Kaycee," she corrected. "Is Mr. Thompson available to see me today?"

Charlotte's eyes traveled over to where Kendrick sat with Martinique. "He's in a meeting right now."

Kaycee turned her head in the direction that Charlotte was looking and her eyes came to rest on Kendrick and Martinique. Her brow raised at the sight of the well-coiffed, sophisticated older woman, and she immediately wished she had chosen something else to wear.

Suddenly the lightweight gray pantsuit and light blue blouse looked rather ordinary compared to the shantung pantsuit that the woman in Kendrick's company was wearing. She hesitated for a moment, not sure if she should approach, but something inside moved her, and before she knew it, she was standing at their table.

Both Kendrick and Martinique looked up simultaneously upon Kaycee's arrival. Kendrick's eyes widened with surprise. He immediately scrambled up from his seat.

"Did we have a meeting today?"

Kaycee shook her head. "No, I was just dropping by to see if you'd come to a decision on that little matter," she said, trying to be as vague as possible. She didn't know the woman sitting at the table and didn't see a reason to be spreading her business.

Martinique gave Kaycee the once-over with a smirk and boldly sat forward in her seat, resting her chin on her crossed hands. Her actions put Kaycee in mind of a lioness claiming her territory.

"About that," Kendrick began. "I think we need to talk."

Kaycee surprised all three of them when she grabbed Kendrick's forearm and said in a sweet voice, "I've been waiting for your response for the last few days. I don't think it's nice to keep me waiting."

Kendrick looked down on her with wide questioning eyes, immediately lost in her beauty. He liked the way her eyes lowered seductively and how her voice was a little over a husky whisper. He liked her soft hands holding on to his arm as though she was more than just a business associate. Her sweet fragrance teased his nostrils.

Was Kaycee trying to come on to him? Martinique's mouth dropped open at Kaycee's boldness, which only delighted Kaycee.

The older woman cleared her throat, breaking through his fantasizing. "Kenny, where are your manners?" she purred with false sweetness.

"Martinique!" Kendrick coughed out. In the midst of Kaycee's actions, he'd forgotten all about their meeting. "I'm sorry, Kaycee Jordan, Martinique Rivers. Kaycee's my, my—" for some reason he was at a loss for words to describe their relationship.

"Good friend," Kaycee threw out in a sugary voice. She reached out her hand for Martinique to shake, but the older woman just stared back in return. It was obvious that she wasn't interested in knowing who Kaycee was.

"Nice to meet you, Kizzy," Martinique said in a bored tone.

"That's *Kaycee,*" Kaycee immediately corrected her.

Knowing Martinique the way he did, Kendrick thought it was best that he separate the two women before some conflict broke out.

"Martinique, please excuse me."

He placed his hand on Kaycee's lower back and led her across the room.

When they were out of earshot of Martinique, he turned to Kaycee with a look of disapproval. "Ms. Jordan, what is going on?"

Kaycee hated that she'd lost her cool; she knew it stemmed from jealousy, but she wasn't about to let Kendrick know that.

"I wanted to know if you'd made your decision about my proposal."

Kendrick stared at her for a few seconds without answering. His response made Kaycee nervous. She didn't know if she could handle him saying no, but she had a feeling that was what she was about to hear.

"Kaycee, I've been thinking about your proposal. I think your business is a great idea and I know that it is something that could definitely enhance my business."

"I feel a *but* coming on," she said softly.

He turned away, not wanting to see disappointment on her beautiful face. "But I'm not sure if it's a good idea that we work together."

"Why's that?" she asked.

He took a few steps forward before turning around to face her. "For starters we're neighbors and we didn't necessarily get off on the right foot. Secondly, I've been in this position before, and I'm not sure if I can trust this kind of arrangement to work again, and third—"

"There's more?" Kaycee asked with a sigh.

Kendrick nodded. "I think you are a beautiful, talented and exciting woman. I don't need any distractions in my life right now."

Kaycee stood there in silence. Had her ears deceived her or did he just say he was distracted by her? She licked her lips and bit down on one of the corners, looking for something to say, but nothing came to mind.

"I wish you well in your endeavors," he said and held out his hand for a shake.

Kaycee placed her hand in his and the same current that had transferred upon their first meeting replayed itself. She shivered in response.

"Good luck to you, too, Kendrick," she whispered. They stood there for a moment, hand in hand, then Kaycee released her hold and walked away.

Holding a glass of chardonnay, Kaycee strolled over to the custom-built wall unit that contained her complete music collection. The cabinet held her compact stereo, vast CD and album collection and her most prized possession, a turntable and microphone given to her by her favorite uncle who'd been a popular deejay.

She fingered through the CDs in search of the right one to complement her mood. The song that came to mind was by one of her favorite artists,

Heather Headley. She smiled when she spotted the CD that contained the song "He Is."

Since her encounter with Kendrick at Café Jireh, she didn't know what to think. His words had both frightened and delighted her. The fact that he didn't want to do business with her was disheartening, but, oddly, his reasons made her hopeful. She'd rather be a distraction than nothing at all!

He made it clear that he was avoiding her. Even she noticed that he had been doing a good job of it by keeping Tiki under wraps and by limiting his time outside where they could bump into each other.

How could she have gotten into a situation like this? All she wanted to do was start up her business. Why did she have to be attracted to her next-door neighbor who owned one of the most popular spots in town in the process? One that she was trying to do business with. Granted, she could go out and try to secure business with other establishments, but everything in the area was practically saturated. Deep down inside, she knew that Jireh and Soulicious were a perfect match.

With a sigh of defeat, Kaycee walked over to the French doors that led out to the lanai. She flipped on the outdoor blue lights and turned on the speakers to the outdoor sound system.

She eased onto the sofa and took a sip of her wine. The June night was beautiful. The air was warm. The moon was a bright orange ball in the sky. It was the kind of night that tempted you to sleep under the stars. Kaycee loved the night air, which was why she'd had the outdoor kitchen and living room added. Any given day or night she'd go outside to sit before the fireplace or prepare dinner in the kitchen.

The slight hum of lawn sprinklers coming on startled her. She watched as the water droplets sprayed across her thick Kentucky blue grass with the precision of a synchronized swim team. It looked so refreshing yet relaxing and seemed to be calling her name.

Kaycee didn't know if it was the alcohol that caused her to make her move. Before she knew it, she'd drunk down the contents of her glass, then she undid the belt on her robe, exposing her tank top and panties underneath. As Heather reached her crescendo in the song, Kaycee boldly walked into the flying spray.

The tepid water cooled her skin as she edged closer to the sprinkler head. There she stood with her eyes closed as the water beat against her body like a thousand tiny massaging hands.

She'd needed to do something crazy to offset the nerves jumping in her stomach. Her life faded in and out of uncertainty and the results haunted her. Four months ago, she'd reassessed and changed her life and she's gotten over the change. Now she was ready to face the results of her decisions.

The midnight shower seemed like just what she needed. Things were going to work out. They had to. She believed that Soulicious was her destiny and she was determined to fulfill it.

As the water pelted her body, Kaycee stood in its midst, totally oblivious to the fact that she was being watched.

Kendrick stood frozen in his bedroom window as he watched Kaycee standing in the sprinklers below. When he had first heard the music, he'd stepped over to the window to investigate just as she was taking off her robe.

He felt wrong for standing there watching her, but he couldn't turn his attention away. Watching Kaycee in action was like studying a piece of fine art. Perfect strokes, the use of color, bold and abstract.

He was sure that if she'd known that his master bedroom faced her backyard, she probably would have thought twice about stepping out like that.

There was nothing lewd about her actions. In fact she looked at ease, at peace, as if the water was refreshing her spirit. In turn, he actually admired her because he didn't know one sister who would do something so spontaneous, especially if it meant getting her hair wet. Martinique surely wouldn't. In this way, Kaycee reminded him of his late wife Amanda.

That she was doing it without knowledge of his observation turned him on.

That was what Kaycee did to him. She didn't know it, but their little verbal exchanges made him want to snatch her up in his arms and press his lips against hers the way he'd seen the men do in old Western movies. She was a definite femme fatale and he was the alpha male. Despite what his head was telling him, he wanted Kaycee Jordan and it would only be a matter of time before he had her.

Chapter 8

"Sid, just say you'll go with me," Kaycee told Sidra over the telephone.

"Where?"

"Just say you'll go, please?" she begged.

"What are you talking about?" Sidra said with a sigh.

"Tonight, I have an important event to attend and I don't want to go by myself."

"What kind of event?" Sidra asked in a bored tone.

"Have you ever heard of Soul Connection?"

"No, what's that?"

"A dating service for black professionals. They're

meeting at Café Jireh tonight and I want you to go with me."

"Ooh," Sidra cooed. "That will mean fine, single brothers with money, girl, count me in!"

"Good, I'll pick you up at seven," Kaycee announced before hanging up the phone.

That was all Kaycee needed. Tonight she was going to show up at Kendrick's affair whether he wanted to work with her or not. She wasn't about to be put off so easily. For some reason, she couldn't cut her losses and walk away. She felt as if she was supposed to pursue this.

She turned on the light in her walk-in closet and went straight to her outfit for the evening: a black halter top with rhinestone beading along the neckline with a matching pair of wide-legged pants that flowed when she walked. She completed the outfit with a pair of stiletto sandals with delicate rhinestone straps.

She wet her hair, applied some mousse to it and spiked it up for a sassy, sexy look. The dramatic style coupled with her smoky eye shadow brought out the natural slant of her eyes. She completed her look with warm gloss on her lips and a natural-toned blush to her cheekbones.

When she looked at herself in the mirror, she smiled as she turned her head from side to side. She looked gorgeous. With a dab of her favorite perfume she was ready to go.

As she backed out of the driveway, a strange feeling came over her. Was she doing the right thing invading Kendrick's party? Was she playing games? What she had admired in the mirror ten minutes earlier, she was ashamed of now. She regretted having asked Sidra to go along because she could see her pouting like a kid leaving a candy store with no purchases if she changed her mind.

She paused at the wheel. It wasn't her style to be so scheming and she thought about pulling back into the garage, but the idea was fleeting as something else overrode her feelings. It was a sense of urgency that was too strong to ignore. She had to be there for him tonight. If only to show her face in support of his efforts, then that was what she would do.

"Sooky, sooky, now," Sidra crooned as she handed over the keys to the handsome young valet.

Kaycee looked at the long line of partygoers. She wished she had arrived earlier. According to her estimations it would easily be more than an hour before they got inside. The thought of standing outside in her finest turned her off. She was a grown woman and had given up waiting in lines to get inside nightclubs years ago.

"Girl," Sidra said through closed teeth, trying not to be too obvious. "I think I died and went to brother heaven! I just hope we don't have to wait in that long line. It could take all night getting through that."

Just as she turned to Sidra to suggest another plan of action, she spotted a familiar face in the crowd. The petite build and fast-paced walk let Kaycee know it was La Jetta. Her eyes lit up. She hadn't seen La Jetta since her first visit. It was like running into an old friend.

"La Jetta!"

La Jetta looked up and let out a shrill of recognition when she saw Kaycee. She scurried over to give her a hug.

"Hey, Kaycee, girl, what is going on besides looking fly?"

"Just let me know when you're ready to give up that outfit," Kaycee replied. La Jetta sported a teal-blue knit top with silver beaded neckline and a tiered skirt paired with silver tie-up stilettos. It was an ensemble that Kaycee could easily see in her own closet.

She nudged her head in the direction of the door. "How's the party?"

"Better now that I got out of there. It's so hot and there's so many people. I just hope they don't tear up the place. Mr. Rick keeps the place nice to draw people, not turn them away, you know."

Kaycee nodded. She hoped Kendrick appreciated that committed staff like La Jetta and Charlotte had his back. They held him in such high esteem that it set a tone for others.

"Charlotte told me you got the meeting."

Kaycee nodded. "I did, thank you so much for your suggestions. It went very well."

"I heard," she replied. "Mr. Rick hasn't stopped talking about you. So when are you going to bring some things in?"

Kaycee didn't answer right away because she was still hung up on La Jetta's words about Kendrick talking about her.

Rather than update her on the conversation that she and Kendrick had had the night before, she just smiled. She guessed that he'd probably been too busy to tell his staff of the latest decision not to partner with her.

"Look, La Jetta, I'd like to go in. Is there any way around the crowd?"

"Yes, there is," she replied. "It's called the Jetta Pass."

She grabbed Kaycee's hand and led her over to the massive bouncer, Sidra tagging along behind. Kaycee's eyes widened as they approached. The bouncer looked as wide as he was tall, with a bald head and a bulldog expression.

"Charles, this is Mr. Rick's new associate. She's here to check out the place."

"No problem, Jet," he replied in a soft voice that

made Kaycee and Sidra exchange glances. Neither could believe that inside that big body resided such a soft voice. It was like Mike Tyson all over again.

"Thanks, La Jetta," Kaycee said. "Are you coming back in?"

La Jetta shook her head with a roll of her eyes. "No, I'm done for the night."

"I'll see you later then."

The moment they entered, Kaycee was surprised and impressed. Gone was the coffee house, replaced by a supper-club environment.

Jireh's was jumping! The transformation of the place had her tongue-tied. What Kaycee had thought would be a tired reception full of bourgeois black folks sipping on champagne and talking about investments and international affairs turned out to be a full-fledged affair with food, a parquet dance floor, live jazz band and outdoor seating, complete with decorative hanging paper lanterns stringing the deck out back. The bar consisted of the usual coffee varieties along with exotic mixed drinks.

Sidra grabbed Kaycee's hand and squeezed it. "Girl, I'm like a kid in a candy store. I don't know if I should eat, buy or what."

Kaycee laughed. Sidra was right. There were some good-looking men in the place. The pair went deeper in the crowd with Sidra pinching Kaycee nearly every time they passed a well-dressed man.

After circling the room, they returned to the front counter to check out the drink menu when Sidra caught sight of two tall men standing off to the side. Both were dressed in casual designer attire, sporting fresh haircuts with bling-bling flashing in their ears and dangling from their necks. To Kaycee they looked like professional basketball players.

"Good evening, ladies," one said, stepping forward and extending his hand. Even in the dim light, Kaycee and Sidra noticed the diamond-encrusted Rolex on his wrist. Sidra, clearly impressed by all that she saw, sashayed over to him, her hips swinging like a pendulum. She extended her hand for him to take.

"Why, hello," she cooed. "Are you having a good time?"

He responded with an equally flirtatious grin, "Now I am."

Sidra giggled in return. "I'm Sidra Rodgers and you are?"

"Hampton Barnes, but my friends call me Hamp," he replied. He turned to his friend standing by his side. "This is my boy, Miles Jordan."

Sidra pulled Kaycee to her side, "What a coincidence. My friend Kaycee's last name is Jordan."

Kaycee looked over at Miles and smiled. "I don't think I see the family resemblance."

"Why do you say that? Because I don't have those

sexy brown eyes?" he asked, leaning down toward her as if trying to get a better look. He was not what Kaycee would call fine, more like cute, with boyish features like Will Smith.

"No, I was thinking more of our trademark foreheads," Kaycee answered. "The hazel eyes actually came from the Harpers on my mom's side."

"But aren't they sexy as hell?" a familiar male voice exclaimed over Kaycee's shoulder. She quickly turned to find herself face-to-face with her ex-fiancé Paul.

Her nose wrinkled in distaste. "Paul," she said with surprise. She hadn't expected to see him. Their months apart appeared to have done him some good. She noticed he was a little slimmer and had grown a mustache; he used to despise facial hair. Yet, he was still the same meticulous, clean-cut Paul down to the tan-and-black shirt, black trousers and sandals.

"Hello, Kaycee." His eyes canvassed the full length of her body before coming to rest on her face.

"Whassup Paul? Is this your playa?" Hampton Barnes asked, jutting his thumb in her direction.

Kaycee immediately decided that she didn't like Hampton.

Paul slyly smiled and slipped his arm around her slim waist. "Yeah, this is my girl."

"Ex-girl," Kaycee quickly corrected him as she

peeled his hand from around her body. She stepped out of his reach. "Get it right."

Her reaction made him flush with embarrassment and he stepped back with an uneasy laugh. "Yeah, that's right."

Miles took the cue and quietly strolled away, taking his attention with him to the next woman standing nearby.

Paul stepped back with a smile, his expression openly lust filled as he admired Kaycee's new look. He shook his head with a click of his tongue.

"My, my, my, Kaycee, I can't get over how good you look. You even changed your hair."

Kaycee stepped back, putting space between them. "I've changed a lot of things in my life, Paul."

"Is that right?"

"Yes," she replied.

"What have you been doing with yourself?"

Kaycee was at a standstill as to what she should say. She debated whether she should tell him about her business venture, but then she remembered how Paul like to intimidate through interrogation, and she thought twice about it. So she was very surprised when Sidra stepped forward to give him the 411.

"My girl here doesn't want to brag, but she's a partner with the owner of this place."

Kaycee rolled her eyes. Leave it to Sidra to make up a fantastic tale and to rub it in his face, too.

Although she didn't agree with telling lies she was glad for Sidra's quick thinking.

"Really?" he asked with a raised brow. "This place is big-time. Congrats."

Kaycee murmured "Thank you," hating that she'd fallen into Sidra's trap, yet glad to be able to show well. Even if it wasn't the truth, at least in Paul's eyes she wasn't sitting around doing nothing after their relationship ended.

"I think this calls for a toast." Paul held up his hand to get the attention of one of the roaming waiters. "What would you like?"

"Nothing, thank you," Kaycee replied, turning to glance around the room again, wondering if Kendrick was nearby. She hadn't seen him when she'd walked around minutes ago.

Her thoughts were interrupted by Paul's hand stroking her hair. Again, she ducked out of his reach and batted his hand away.

"Stop it, Paul," she said with irritation.

"Sidra, why's your girl acting all scared of me?" Paul asked. "It's not like we don't know each other."

"I don't know, Paul, but I will have a Key Lime Margarita," Sidra shouted out her order. "With extra lime."

"Baby, I got your drink," Hampton informed her with a tug on her arm. Sidra responded by sinking back against him suggestively.

"What do you want, Kaycee?" Paul asked, getting back to her order. "Do you still drink Cosmopolitans like they're going out of style?"

Kaycee shook her head. "No, that's a thing of my past, too." She hoped he caught on to the double meaning.

However, Paul was not fazed. "So, what do you drink now?"

"I think a glass of white wine will suit the lady just fine," a husky male voice intervened. The quartet turned around to find Kendrick standing behind them.

Kaycee's heart began to thump rapidly in her chest, and she fought to keep the excitement of seeing him out of her face. He was dashing in a crisp white shirt and tailored black trousers.

"Kendrick, hi," she said, just above a whisper.

"Kaycee," he leaned over and kissed her on the cheek. What could have been viewed as a greeting between associates was much more between the two of them.

Their closeness sent Kaycee's senses spiraling so that she had to lean against the counter to steady herself lest she sink to the floor.

Out of the corner of her eye, Kaycee noticed Paul's stunned expression. But she didn't care.

Sidra cleared her throat and tapped Kaycee on the arm. "Did you say Kendrick? As in your neighbor?"

Kaycee just nodded.

Sidra gave him the once-over. "*You're* the neighbor?" she exclaimed.

Kendrick took Sidra's hand in his "It's nice to see you again."

"You sure clean up well."

Kendrick chuckled and remarked to the group, "If you all will excuse us, I need to meet with Ms. Jordan briefly." He placed his palm at the small of her back and had begun to lead her away when Paul stepped between them.

"Excuse me, *pops,* but the lady and I were having a conversation."

He stood tall with his chest puffed out like a rooster readying himself for an attack.

"I'm sorry, *son,*" Kendrick retorted, emphasizing the word as Paul had. He looked down at Kaycee. "Ms. Jordan, did I interrupt anything? I can always meet with you later."

Kaycee's eyes locked with his and her stomach fluttered. The last place she wanted to be was left with Paul. Kendrick was more potent than any drink. "No, we can meet now," she softly replied.

"Good," Kendrick repositioned his hand around her waist. He looked back at Paul. "Now, if you would excuse us."

Paul glowered but stepped out of their way without another word.

Kaycee just shrugged as Kendrick guided her through the throngs of people. As they made their way toward the back office, Kendrick heard his name being called. He turned around to find Wallace and Lynn Dennis, owners of a popular community newspaper. The pair were obviously covering the event for their next issue, as they were ready with camera and pen and pad in hand.

"Ken, can we get a photo and an interview for the paper?" Wallace asked, stopping Kendrick with a hand on his shoulder.

Although he was eager to get Kaycee alone, Kendrick graciously complied. He guided Kaycee by the elbow to his side, hoping that she got the idea that he didn't want her to leave. The knowing look she gave him let him know that she didn't intend to.

With a confident smile, he replied, "Sure."

Lynn began running off a slew of questions about the purpose of the event and what business had been like since the grand opening.

Kaycee stood by and listened as Kendrick responded with poise and confidence. She felt proud standing by his side during his celebrity moment.

The questioning ended, Wallace asked for a photo opportunity. Kaycee had started to move away when she felt a light tap on her shoulder. She glanced back to find Kendrick signaling her to return to his side.

"I shouldn't be in the photo," she informed him.

"Yes, you should," he replied. "It will make the picture look more lively."

Kaycee returned to her spot beside him and stood smiling awkwardly. She didn't know where to put her hands or how close to stand to Kendrick.

As Wallace and Lynn departed, Kaycee felt Kendrick's arm move from her lower back to completely encircle her waist. This time he led her straight to his office.

The back area consisted of Kendrick's office, a second smaller office, a restroom and a common room that served as both the staff break room and a boardroom. Kendrick headed for his office.

Kaycee was surprised to see that the room was sterile and lacked the personality and vibe of the rest of the building. The light gray office contained an oversized desk with matching credenza, two chairs and a bookshelf. There were no pictures, no plaques, nothing.

Kendrick walked around to the other side of the desk and sat in the leather executive chair.

"Ms. Jordan..." he began.

"Ms. Jordan?" Kaycee repeated. "Are we back to formalities again? Just a minute ago, I was Kaycee."

He sighed in admission to her response. "Kaycee, why are you here tonight?"

She was stumped by his question. "Should I not have come?"

"I'm not saying that," he said, rubbing his temples to relieve the building tension. "I just didn't expect you here tonight."

Kaycee felt like a child about to face punishment in the principal's office. She shifted her stance. "I came to support you," she replied. "Is that a crime?"

Kendrick looked up and fell into the amber warmth of her eyes. "No it's not. Thank you."

"You're welcome," she replied with a dimpled smile and wink.

"Since you're here I may as well ask how you think the place looks," he said.

"I think it looks nice. I really haven't seen much because you came and snatched me out of the crowd."

His eyes dropped to take in her full form down to her perfectly painted toes, and he nodded in appreciation. "You look nice this evening."

"Thank you," she politely replied. His inspection was seducing. "So do you."

"Did you hear your friend's comment?" he asked, speaking of Sidra. "I guess I *can* clean up real nice."

Kaycee snickered. "You'll have to excuse Sidra, she can be a little forward sometimes."

"I guess the fruit doesn't fall too far—" A sharp voice pierced through the room.

Their conversation broke as they both turned to the doorway to find a heated Martinique. The look on her face and black slinky outfit put Kaycee in mind of Morticia, the mother of the Addams Family.

Kendrick stood from his chair. "Martinique—"

"Kendrick, don't bother," she said slithering into the room. "I came here to help you pull this evening off and you embarrass me by entertaining this—" she scanned Kaycee with a look of disgust. "—this tart."

"Wait a minute—" Kaycee began.

"Martinique!" Kendrick boomed. "This is neither the time nor the place."

"It sure isn't," she scoffed. "I'm leaving!" She turned on her heel and marched out of the room like a two-year-old having a temper tantrum.

Kendrick ran behind her. "Martinique!"

It had happened so fast that Kaycee didn't know what to think, let alone do. She took a seat and hoped that Kendrick could resolve things and bring Martinique back, but when he returned alone fifteen minutes later, she knew that things had not gone well.

"Kendrick, what happened?" she exclaimed jumping up from her chair.

He shook his head. "Martinique walked out on me and we haven't even started serving dinner. I don't know why she was tripping, it's not like you and I were doing anything."

She eased down on the corner of his desk.

"Are you seeing Martinique?" she whispered,

wanting to know the level of their relationship while hoping not to hear the word *yes*.

"No," he replied.

Kaycee exhaled with relief.

"A few years back, we used to date, but now it's strictly a business relationship."

Kaycee licked her lips. "She acts like she's still in love with you."

"I don't know why," he grumbled. The only woman he was finding himself drawn to was the one standing in front of him. "We haven't seen each other for more than a year."

"Why did you break up?"

"She just wasn't the one. I think you know the one when you meet her."

The room was silent for a few moments as both pondered Kendrick's last words. It was Kaycee who broke the silence. She stood up and smoothed out her dress.

"Where do you need me to start?"

Kendrick's brow raised. "Excuse me?"

"Martinique is gone and, like you said, you have folks to feed."

"Kaycee, you don't have to—" he began.

"I know I don't have to," she replied, then softly added. "I want to."

Her words caused his insides to leap, and he thought he could easily have cleared off his desktop and made her his right then. The thought made the blood rush from his brain to his lower regions, and he stumbled on his response.

"Uh…uh, to the kitchen I guess," he said and rushed from the room. The gentleman in him would have allowed her to exit the room first, but he didn't want to catch another glimpse of her backside or he would be totally at her mercy.

The whole evening went off without a hitch. Kaycee proved herself to be invaluable as she aided Kendrick in pulling off a great event.

She informed Sidra that she would be catching a ride with Kendrick since she would be working. Sidra was happy because that meant she could follow Hampton to check out another party without having to worry about getting Kaycee home. To her relief, Kaycee didn't see Paul again the rest of the night. She wanted to put on her best face to prove to Kendrick that they could work together. She played hostess by engaging in conversations with community leaders and political figures, all of which she enjoyed immensely.

A little after one o'clock, the crowd began to thin along with Kaycee's patience with the discomfort she was feeling from her aching feet.

The band began to wind down their last set with a saxophone rendition of Etta James's song "At Last." Her sentiments in line with the song, Kaycee crawled into a booth and kicked off her sandals. She yawned as she massaged her stiff toes and the numb balls of her feet. The shoes were cute, but not to work in.

Kendrick was standing by the door talking to three other men. The four could easily have been discussing anything from politics to coffee as far as Kaycee could tell. All of them were "seasoned" with age and were equally handsome, but it was Kendrick who stood out. She knew he was an older man, but compared to the others he looked more virile.

His back was strong and broad and looked as though it could withstand heavy weights. His defined arms promised to pick her up and hold her closely with ease. She was sure the rest of him wasn't small-time, either.

As if Kendrick knew she was checking him out, he glanced over his shoulder with a smile. From the look on his face, she thought he had read her mind, like Mel Gibson in the movie *What A Woman Wants*. She blushed, turning away quickly.

He shook the other men's hands and headed over to the booth.

"Ms. Jordan, I owe you big-time," he said, sliding in the booth beside her.

"Yes, you do, and you can start by rubbing my feet," she said playfully lifting her leg.

Kendrick surprised her by taking her foot and placing it in his lap where he proceeded to massage the pain away.

His hands worked miracles and she found herself succumbing to his touch. She leaned back in the booth and closed her eyes, moaning with pleasure.

"You like that?" Kendrick whispered, watching her face.

"Ye-e-es," she purred with a delicious smile.

"How much?"

"A lot."

"Tell me then. Tell me you like it," he coaxed as his fingertips began to knead deeper into the center of her foot.

"I like it," she murmured. "I definitely like it."

"Tell me again."

"I like it," she repeated not thinking about how her confession might sound to the few people still milling about.

Although Kendrick was well aware of where he was taking her, he stopped stroking her immediately.

Kaycee's eyes popped open. "Why did you stop? It felt good."

"Listen to us," he replied. "It's a good thing no one is in earshot or they might think we're doing something else under this table." He gently replaced her foot on the floor. "Ms. Jordan, if you're ready, I think I'd better get you home."

Kaycee couldn't agree more and quickly gathered her sandals and purse in hand. After Kendrick gave the final directives to his staff, they headed out to his car.

It wasn't until they stepped out onto the front sidewalk that Kendrick spotted Kaycee's shoes dangling by their straps from her fingers.

He frowned. "Why aren't you wearing your shoes?" he asked gruffly.

"My feet were about to declare war if I didn't take them off." She sighed.

His furrowed brow raised and he said, "I'm not going to say a word, but this is like déjà vu."

Kaycee rolled her eyes at his reference to the night of their first meeting and his comment about her shoes. The image of him standing in his doorway without a shirt, his muscles flexing, made her warm. She was grateful for the gentle evening breeze ruffling the skirt of her dress. She closed her eyes and sighed, letting the wind cool her flushed skin.

Standing beside her, Kendrick watched in awe. While she was enjoying the fresh air, he could not help but be reminded of that night he'd seen her playing in the sprinklers from his bedroom window. And just like that night, his body responded instantly. He couldn't understand it, but there was something about Kaycee that left him speechless.

A single raindrop splattering his forehead brought him back to the present. He reached up to wipe it away only to be hit by another and another. The drops quickly formed a design on his shirt. He looked up into the starless sky and frowned.

"It's raining."

"Oh, no," she replied, huddling beside him. "I didn't bring an umbrella."

Lightning zigzagged across the sky, followed by a low rumble of thunder. The droplets increased and before Kendrick could reply, the wind picked up.

"We're going to have to make a run for it," he announced.

"Wait," Kaycee replied, coming to a halt. "Let me put on my shoes."

"We don't have time for that!" he barked with authority and as quick as the lightning flickering across the sky, he scooped Kaycee up in his arms and made a break for his car.

By the time he reached his Jeep, the rain was pouring down in buckets. Somehow, he maneuvered the door open and practically tossed Kaycee inside before jumping in behind her. Breathless and drenched, the laughing pair fell against the seats before taking a good look at each other.

Kendrick's shirt clung to his body almost like a second skin, while Kaycee looked like a contestant in a wet T-shirt contest with her dress molding against her breasts and thighs, revealing the outline of her feminine curves.

For a moment, it was as if they were suspended in time. Both were fighting the urge to look away but neither was doing so. Kendrick stared as Kaycee's mouth parted unconsciously. Her soft, moist lips reminded him of ripe strawberries, making him want to lean over and taste their sweetness. For a moment he almost did that…until he came to his senses.

Clearing his throat, he turned away and started the engine.

"Clearly this night has spiraled well beyond both of our expectations," he announced.

His comment came from nowhere and his change in demeanor made her uncomfortable. She crossed her arms protectively before her chest, hiding the tight buds that had formed from the cold rain. Without a word, she turned to look out the passenger window. She didn't know what was going on or why.

All she knew was that she had grown quite fond of Kendrick Thompson. She knew that she liked being around him, and frankly, she wanted to know more. Kendrick had ignited flames that were getting harder to extinguish each day.

She sighed and inhaled the smell of his cologne clinging to her dress. She closed her eyes and leaned back, savoring the physical closeness they had just shared.

The ride home was silent. It wasn't until Kendrick turned onto their block that Kaycee looked over at the profile of the man sitting beside her and she shivered from the attraction. He embodied everything that said *strong black man.*

"Kendrick, what did you mean about things spiraling beyond our expectations?"

Kendrick put the Jeep in Park but kept the engine running. He leaned back with a deep sigh and ran his hand over his head. He remained still for a moment, choosing his words carefully. In order for them to work successfully together their relationship had to remain professional. Their obvious attraction to one another had to diminish.

"Kaycee, I appreciate the way you jumped in tonight after Martinique left."

"No problem," she coolly replied and reached for the door handle.

"No one has ever come through for me like that before. You really helped to make this evening successful and I want to thank you."

"It's okay, Kendrick, I would have done the same for anybody."

He shook his head in disagreement. "But the point is that you didn't have to, yet you did, and I would like to know one thing."

"What's that?"

"Kaycee, would you like to work with me at Jireh?"

His words sound more like a marriage proposal than a job offer. And her response echoed an acceptance. "You know I'd love to."

He hit the steering wheel with the palm of his hand. "Then it's settled. I'll see you at ten tomorrow."

"That's it?" she asked.

"That's it, unless you have something to say."

"Thank you for the opportunity, Kendrick," she softly replied. "I promise I won't let you down."

He got out of the Jeep on his side and pulled out his umbrella from the back. Walking around to Kaycee's side, he opened her door and, like a gentleman, escorted her up the walk.

Kaycee thought his actions were not necessary but appreciated the chivalrous treatment all the same. It really made her feel special.

He took her keys from her hands and opened her door.

"I'll see you tomorrow," he said and placed the keys in her palm.

"Okay," she replied, stepping inside.

As he went down the walk, he couldn't help but think what he would give to be a fly on her bedroom wall when she took off those wet clothes. He waited until he saw lights come on before backing out of the driveway, all the while hoping that he wasn't making a mistake.

Chapter 9

"Welcome to Café Jireh!" La Jetta greeted Kaycee as she always did when a customer entered. The minute she realized who it was, she shrieked for joy and scurried from behind the counter.

"Welcome to the family!" she exclaimed, giving Kaycee a hug.

"Thanks, La Jetta, that means so much," Kaycee said smiling.

Still holding Kaycee's hands, La Jetta stepped back to examine her outfit. "Now you know, orange is my favorite color."

"Do you think this is too much?" Kaycee asked,

hoping that she wasn't too overdressed in the thin wrap sweater, beige skirt and low-heeled mules. Although casual, she felt more dressed up in comparison to La Jetta's uniform of cotton khaki pants and company-emblazoned polo top.

La Jetta shook her head, "Girl, you are fine. At Jireh we allow everyone to be who they are—you'll see."

Kaycee glanced at her watch. Kendrick had said to report at 10:00 a.m. and it was now 9:50 a.m. She'd made sure to be a little early. "So where do I go?"

"Oh, let me show you around and introduce you to the crew."

La Jetta guided her to the dining room where a gangly dreadlock-wearing young man was wiping down tables.

"Hey Jaylen, let me introduce you to the newest member of our staff."

Jaylen turned at the sound of his name and smiled.

"Kaycee, what's your last name again?" La Jetta asked.

"Jordan," Kaycee said, realizing that she and La Jetta hadn't been formally introduced when they'd first met.

"Jaylen, this is Ms. Jordan. She'll be providing the baked goods for us and doing some other things. Kaycee, Jaylen Harrison. Jaylen busses tables and waits on customers. He only works part-time because he's in college at Georgia State. He's got his eyes set on being an attorney, and we all have no doubt that he'll make a great one."

Kaycee extended her hand. "It's nice to meet you, Jaylen, but please, call me Kaycee."

"It's nice to meet you, too, Miss Kaycee," he replied, shaking her hand firmly.

Kaycee cringed at the title *Miss* being added to her name. It made her feel older than her approaching thirtieth birthday.

After La Jetta gave her a tour, she took her back to the kitchen. It was small, but very efficient, with state-of-the-art appliances and ample work space. Just enough to do what she needed.

She immediately noticed a bristly-faced old man standing by the grill barking out orders to a middle-aged Hispanic man and a young woman who looked to be in her twenties. They all looked up when they spotted Kaycee.

"Hey y'all!" La Jetta called out. "What's going on?"

"Nothing but you, Jetta," the old man replied with a wink.

"That's what you say today and tomorrow you'll be trying to get me fired."

The young girl burst out laughing and quickly covered her mouth.

"Hey, let me introduce you all to Mr. Rick's new associate."

They all gathered at the cutting station.

"This is Kaycee Jordan. She's going to be doing the desserts for Jireh from now on, as well as assisting Mr. Rick in planning events."

Kaycee gave La Jetta a sidelong glance at the mention of her event-planning skills. Kendrick must have really talked to her in detail.

La Jetta placed her hand on the shoulder of the older man who reminded Kaycee of a little George Jefferson with gray hair.

"Kaycee this is Otis, our house chef," La Jetta announced proudly.

"Chef!" Otis blared out. "I ain't nuttin' but the cook!"

"Otis, what did we tell you about minimizing yourself?" La Jetta chastised. "Mr. Rick gave you the title of chef, so walk in it."

He mumbled something under his breath and waved La Jetta off before offering his wrist to Kaycee. "I would shake your hand, but I've been handling some meat and I don't want to get you messy, but welcome."

"Thank you," Kaycee replied with a smile. He might have a bark, but Otis's thoughtfulness made her like him right away.

La Jetta turned to the other two. "This is Rafael, the sous chef, and Melody, the assistant."

"It's good meeting you both," Kaycee said with a smile.

Rafael responded in kind. Melody only nodded

while holding her hand over her mouth. Kaycee later learned from La Jetta that the girl covered her mouth because she'd been in a bad automobile accident a couple of years back and had lost most of her front teeth. As a result, she was shy about smiling around strangers.

The tour ended at Kendrick's small office.

"Mr. Rick is out running errands," La Jetta announced and picked up a manila folder left on the table. "He told me to give you this to read through and fill out the appropriate paperwork and he'll see you when he gets back this afternoon."

Kaycee nodded and set her things down. With a happy sigh, she sat down and opened the folder.

"Hey, is somebody hungry in here?"

Kaycee glanced up from her place at the desk to find La Jetta standing in the doorway with a tray in hand.

"Am I?" she said, rubbing her growling stomach.

La Jetta carried over the tray and set it on the desk. The French onion soup, smoked mozzarella and cheddar grilled cheese sandwich and Caesar salad looked very appetizing along with a glass of sweet tea on ice.

"It's on the house," La Jetta said, removing the items from the tray and placing them before her.

Kaycee's eyes lit up with appreciation at the deliciously prepared meal. "Thank you so much."

"Oh, don't thank me, Mr. Rick asked me to bring it in to you. He felt badly about not being here on your first day and thought it was the least he could do."

Kaycee glanced at her watch and was surprised to see that it was after two o'clock. "Wow, the time has flown by."

"You should have been in the dining room at lunchtime. It was a madhouse!" La Jetta pulled a straw from her apron pocket and handed it to Kaycee before leaning over the contents of the folder she gave her earlier. "What has he got you reading?"

"Everything I wanted to know about coffee and cafés. It's pretty interesting."

"Don't be surprised if he gives you a pop quiz."

The surprised look on Kaycee's face made La Jetta burst into a fit of giggles.

"Relax, girl, I'm just kidding. Mr. Rick can be no-nonsense, but he's a very nice guy."

Kaycee took a bite of the sandwich and rolled her eyes back into her head. "Oh, my goodness, this is *so* good!"

"I'll let Otis know."

"Is he married?" she asked, taking another bite. "Because I could use a man like him around my house."

"A marriage proposal from a sandwich? Is that all you got to do these days?" a voice asked from behind.

Both women turned to find Kendrick standing in the open doorway. Kaycee's eyes shone at the sight of him. He looked both sexy and powerful in a pin-striped shirt and neutral tie with dark blue tailored trousers. His clean-scented cologne filled the room like an aphrodisiac, making her tongue-tied. She was grateful for La Jetta's presence, as well as for the food before her to act as a buffer until she regained her composure.

"Hey, Mr. Rick, I'm about to take off," La Jetta announced, walking toward the door.

"Thanks for holding down the fort, Jetta," he said, his eyes glued on Kaycee. "It looks great out there."

"No problem, I'll see y'all tomorrow," she said, and headed for the door.

"Hey, Jetta, is Charlotte on her way in?"

La Jetta spun around on her heel. "Nope. Remember she has the night off to go to her son's graduation from the police academy?"

Kendrick slapped his forehead with his opened palm.

"Oh, I completely forgot, who do we have working tonight?"

"Jaylen is here until five and John and Nichole will be in at six."

"I guess I'll have to go out there with Jaylen."

"I can help, too, you know," Kaycee piped up.

"Is that so?" Kendrick replied. "Everybody who goes on the floor must have finished reading the training materials."

Kaycee patted the folder beside her. "I'm done."

Kendrick's brow raised with skepticism. "You finished reading all of that?"

"Yep," she proudly replied.

Kendrick reached for the folder. "Good, then let me quiz you."

"Didn't I tell you?" La Jetta said with a laugh. "Let me get out of here, I got to pick up my boys."

"Okay, Jet, see ya tomorrow," Kendrick called out.

When La Jetta finally departed, Kendrick dropped down in the empty chair opposite Kaycee and brought one leg up to rest his ankle atop his knee.

For a few seconds, he watched Kaycee eat her sandwich. She bit into the gooey center of one of the sandwich halves and pulled it away leaving a trail of cheese that fell down her chin.

She laughed. "Not only is this the best grilled cheese sandwich that I ever had, but it's fun to eat, too."

"I'll be sure to tell Otis," he replied in amusement.

"So what's been keeping you out of the office all day?" she asked.

Kendrick noticed a piece of mozzarella sticking to her chin. He leaned over the desk and gently smoothed it away with the tip of his thumb, leaving a burning sensation in the pit of Kaycee's stomach from his touch.

Totally unaware of the effect he had on her, Kendrick sank back in his seat with a sigh. "I had to visit vendors."

"Sounds like fun."

"I'm glad you think that, maybe I can give you that responsibility to handle, as well."

"Hey, I don't mind. I actually had some ideas I wanted to share with you anyway," she stated, pushing her plate to the side. She reached for her briefcase and placed it on the desktop. She removed two packets in clear protective sleeves and handed one to Kendrick.

"I was thinking of the different types of promotions that we could hold here to stand out against your competitors. I did some research and took it upon myself to jot down some ideas, tell me what you think."

Kendrick read through the first page. When he turned to the second page, his eyes widened at the fifteen suggested events, followed by complete detailed descriptions of each.

When he didn't comment, Kaycee began to explain her suggestions.

"I was thinking that if we established ourselves as a place where local authors can hold book signings and book clubs hold discussions, we can pull in the type of crowd that would really appreciate a coffeehouse setting."

Kendrick read silently without even glancing up, which made Kaycee try another angle.

"I was also thinking that you could host a poetry

or spoken-word night or have live jazz once a month. That group that you had at the event last night was great—maybe they could be like the house band or something."

She paused to give Kendrick a chance to jump in, but he made no move. Swallowing hard, she continued on.

"Now, the salsa lessons will be the most unique twist to the setup. We can offer free lessons once a month on a Saturday morning and then actual dancing later that same evening. I can see even decorating the place with a Latin vibe then—"

"Whoa, hold up," Kendrick interrupted in a booming voice. "Book signings, spoken word, Salsa lessons—this is a respectable establishment, not the place for that kind of bourgeois stuff."

Kaycee was surprised by his response. She'd expected him to be just as excited about her ideas as she was in coming up with them, but it was just the opposite. Concern lined her face. The butterflies she'd had moments earlier when he entered the room fluttered away and were now replaced by a ton of disappointing bricks.

"Bourgeois stuff? Kendrick, what exactly are you saying?"

"I—I'm just saying that it really doesn't take all of this," he stood up. "When I came up with Jireh's concept, I had a vision in mind. It wasn't to try and attract the rich and famous, it was to be a relaxing environment for ordinary people to come for good food and peace of mind. All of this is just too commercial for me."

"What's so commercial about it?" Kaycee asked.

"Book signings, spoken word. I don't want Jireh to be perceived as that. It might sound good now, but in a few months, the crowds will dwindle when something new comes along and then what will we do?"

"What are you talking about, Kendrick?" Kaycee asked. "Jireh is doing well. You already have a strong customer base. We would be building on the solid foundation that you already established."

"You said it right there, Ms. Jordan. The solid foundation that *I* already established. I don't see where we need to fix anything."

His emphasis on the word *I* let Kaycee know that she had crossed the line.

"I'm sorry, I wasn't implying that Jireh needed fixing. I was just offering some ideas. New things don't have to be so painful, you know." She picked up the packets and placed them into her briefcase. "Mr. Thompson, I don't know what you expected from me, but if you really didn't want my services then why did you hire me?"

"Good question!" he barked.

Both paused as his words penetrated the atmosphere and lingered in the air like a smelly fart.

Kaycee shook her head and closed her briefcase. "I guess that said it all. Have a good day, Mr. Thompson!" She marched past him and out the door.

Chapter 10

Kaycee calmly walked to her car.

As she reached inside her purse for her keys, she pulled out a bright-yellow slip of paper. Scrawled across it in Sidra's handwriting was the name and number of her friend, Grant Craddock.

Since that day, Kaycee hadn't thought twice about Grant.

She held up the phone number as if to recall any standout qualities that Sidra may have rattled off, when the Black Business Network came to mind.

A smile curved her mouth as she thought of all the potential business she could gain there for her business. The network's membership consisted of well-off, successful black entrepreneurs in the Greater Atlanta area. With a new surge of purpose, she immediately located her keys and unlocked her car. Once inside its confines she dialed Grant's number.

The line rang twice before his voice mail picked up.

"You've reached Grant. At the sound of the tone, please leave me a detailed message and I will return your call. Peace."

Kaycee liked the sound of his voice right off. It was both clear and friendly. She liked the way he enunciated each word like a radio disc jockey with a laid-back flair. She wondered if the short, to-the-point greeting was indicative of his personality.

Beep!

"Uh, Grant, this is Sidra's friend, Kaycee Jordan. I'm just calling to…touch base. Yes, to touch base with you. Sidra said you should expect my call. Anyway, give me a call back when you get a chance."

She gave her number and snapped her cell phone shut then shook her head, hoping that she didn't sound like a complete idiot. With a backward glance at Café Jireh, Kaycee sighed with disappointment at what could have been.

The warm evening was the perfect weather to enjoy a bowl of ice cream before the television. After taking a shower, Kaycee smoothed some shea butter on her skin and slipped into her pajama short set.

She slipped a pair of footies onto her feet before descending the stairs and heading into the kitchen. Turning on the light, she made a beeline for the freezer and the container of Moose Tracks ice cream that awaited her.

When she grabbed the container, she grimaced at its light weight. Fearing the worse, she pulled it out and looked inside to find nothing more than a spoonful left.

"Sid!" she groaned, recalling the image of her friend eating out of the container at her last visit. The girl had a stomach like a bottomless pit yet never seemed to gain a pound!

Had she been in the mood, she would have whipped up something quick from her collection of recipes, but she didn't have the energy. Besides, the night was a lazy one for her, which was a rarity.

She quickly scanned the remaining odds and ends in the refrigerator. There wasn't enough of anything there to make a decent dessert. Empty-handed, she was trudging into the family room when the doorbell rang.

The clock overhead read 8:47 p.m. She never got visitors so late in the evening. The only person who would dare was Sidra, but even she wouldn't come clear across town without calling first.

Peeking out the peephole, Kaycee was surprised

to find Kendrick standing there with bags in his hands. Her heart raced as she wondered what he wanted. Especially after the harsh words spoken earlier that day in his office, Kaycee hadn't expected to see him again—at least not on purpose.

Crossing her arms before her, she leaned against the door. She had a good mind to leave him standing there after the way he'd driven her from the café earlier that day. However, curiosity won out, and, without a thought as to what she was wearing, Kaycee unlocked and opened the door.

Only when she saw the look of awe on Kendrick's face did she remember her scantily clad appearance, and she jumped behind the door.

"Kendrick!" she exclaimed, flushing. "What are you doing here?"

"I—I had some leftover food from the restaurant and thought you might be hungry," he said, holding up the bags.

"As you can see, I didn't expect any visitors," she apologized. "Can you give me a second to cover up?"

"I didn't mean to just barge over, I can leave," he began and leaned over to set the bags on the porch.

"No!" she blurted, her sudden outburst causing him to freeze. "I mean, it's okay. Just give me a second, okay?"

"Sure," he replied.

Kaycee partially closed the door and took the

steps two at a time before scurrying across the landing to her bedroom where she located her dark purple satin robe. It was the first cover-up that she could find. Although it was made of a different material, the purple toned well with her lavender pajamas.

Breathless, she reappeared at the door with a smile.

"Now, what is this here? A peace offering of sorts?"

Kendrick chuckled. "Yes, I guess you can say so."

"Then, by all means, come inside," she said stepping aside to let him enter.

He waited for her to lead the way. Although their homes were similar in layout, their choices in upgrades differed, as did their taste in decor.

The empty formal living room lay to his left, and the room to the immediate left of the entrance, which he used as his home office, was some sort of library in her home. He could tell by the tall oak bookcases filled with hundreds of books, the plush royal-purple chaise lounge and the Tiffany-style reading lamp.

They continued back into the large open kitchen where he sat the bags on the countertop. Again, the layout was similar, with crown molding above the cabinets, stainless-steel appliances and an oversized island in the center of the room, however, the difference lay again in their choices of colors and textures. Kaycee's cabinets were honey-walnut with sand-colored granite countertops and ceramic-tile flooring while he preferred cherrywood cabinets with black marble countertops and hardwood flooring.

"I like your place," he said looking around.

"Thanks. The only rooms I've been able to work on are the family room and my bedroom. I guess those are the only rooms I care about."

Her confession tickled his curiosity, making him want to see her secret domain.

The rumbling of her stomach came on cue, reminding her that she hadn't eaten since she was at the café. She peeked inside the bags to find a loaf of French bread, two bowls of bistro steak salad and two pieces of her sweet-potato cheesecake.

"Where do you want me to put this?" Kendrick asked, holding up a bottle of white wine.

"Now, I don't recall that being on Jireh's menu, but you can find the wineglasses in the cabinet behind you."

He retrieved the glasses and located the corkscrew, as well. After opening the bottle, he poured two healthy glasses and opened the refrigerator to place the bottle inside. What he saw astounded him.

"Kaycee!"

"What?" Kaycee shrieked, rushing to his side.

"Where is your food?" he asked, eyeing the practically bare box.

She waved his question off and returned to opening the bags. "There's food in there."

"Yeah, for a rabbit," he retorted holding up a cucumber and a bag of wilted spinach salad. "Why don't you have any food?"

"I have food. Just enough for me."

"That is not food," he replied. "Where's your milk and eggs?"

"I'm lactose intolerant and I hate eggs," she answered.

Kendrick shook his head, not accepting her excuse. "Kaycee, you of all people know what it means to have the essentials on hand. Don't forget, you're in the restaurant business."

"Am I?" she asked bluntly, finding the perfect opportunity to know where she stood with him.

With a tilt of his head, Kendrick contritely replied. "If you'll change your mind and forgive me for being a jerk, I would like you to remain at Café Jireh."

His apology made her give in quite easily. "Just don't let it happen again," she playfully warned, her balled fist drawing a smile from him.

Kendrick carried the salad and bread while Kaycee took the wine and glasses into the family room where Kaycee turned on the television.

A familiar red bullet hole covered the screen like a bloodstained target. A figure walked into the center and turned sharply, shooting his gun.

"Aw, shoot," Kendrick called out, hurrying to sit down on the sofa.

Kaycee's brow raised. "What? You don't like Bond?"

"Are you kidding? He's my boy."

Kaycee's mouth dropped open in amazement. She didn't know many men who liked James Bond movies. Paul had said they were just as fake as WWF wrestling and had refused to watch them with her.

She placed the glasses on the table. "I'm the biggest James Bond fan."

"Yeah, next to me," Kendrick replied.

"Oh, yeah, let's see how much you know," she challenged.

He waved her off, "You don't want to test me, I don't want to embarrass you by getting all the questions right," he teased.

Kaycee's eyes lit up with excitement as her mind raked through James Bond trivia like lightning. "Oh, we'll see about that!" she crowed.

Marching in front of the television, she placed her hands on her hips. "Are you ready Mr. Know-Every-thing-About-Bond?"

"Okay, you asked for it," he replied and took a bite of salad. "Hit me with your best shot."

"Question number one: What was the first Bond movie?"

"That's easy," he snorted with a wave of his hand. "It was Dr. No."

Kaycee nodded with approval. "Okay, how many James Bonds have there been?"

"Six. Sean Connery, George Lazenby, Roger Moore, Timothy Dalton, Pierce Brosnan and they recently signed on a new guy, Daniel Craig."

"Okay, Mr. Big Shot, here's a hard one. Which two movies did the villain Jaws appear in?"

Kendrick faked a yawn, "*Moonraker* and *The Spy Who Loved Me.*"

"Who is the only Bond girl to appear in more than one Bond film?"

"Easy, Maude Adams. She played in *Octopussy* and *The Man with the Golden Gun,* and she was an extra in *A View to Kill.*"

"Okay, okay, you know a little something," she conceded, reclaiming her spot on the sofa.

"You're pretty good, though," Kendrick replied, impressed by her knowledge. "What does a young girl like you got business watching James Bond movies?"

"My brothers and I have been fans since we were kids. We used to pretend play Bond all the time. My oldest brother Rusty always played Felix. My brother Mark played Q because he liked showing off the gadgets. The villain was Darren because he is the most devious, while the baby, Kyle was Bond himself. I played both the Bond girl and Moneypenny."

Laughter rippled through the room and before

Kaycee knew it, Kendrick was holding his sides. "Moneypenny? Moneypenny?"

Kaycee pushed him over on the couch. "Whatever! I was the only one who had two roles."

"I see where you get your creativity from."

She began picking through her salad. "Speaking of creativity, are you sure you don't want to reconsider some of my ideas?"

He eased back on the leather cushions. "You know, I thought about it and I must admit your suggestions were all good. I just couldn't see how they fit with the Jireh concept. Then I realized that I hadn't shared my vision of how Jireh came to be."

"You didn't, but I would love to hear it," she replied, drawing her legs up on the sofa.

Kendrick placed his fork on his plate and sat back.

"It was actually the brainchild of my wife Amanda. She had a dream of owning a coffee house when Seattle's Best Coffee and later Starbucks became popular on the coasts. But she wanted the offerings to reflect our culture. For two years, we put together a business plan. We got the schematics drawn up, purchased the business license, the whole shebang. When we were done, we looked around and we didn't have a dime."

He laughed and Kaycee could see him losing himself in reflections of the past.

"Amanda was a woman of true faith. While our

bank accounts said, not right now, she believed God said now. She was the one who came up with the name Café Jireh. *Jireh* means God is our provider. Amanda believed it was the Lord who reminded us of an old treasury note that I purchased years ago. When I redeemed the note, it was exactly what we needed.

"Right about the time that we were going to put something down on a location, Amanda was diagnosed with stage-three ovarian cancer. She was gone a year later.

"So, I picked up and left California to be closer to my daughter Bianca."

"I'm sorry about your wife," Kaycee solemnly replied.

Clasping his hands together, Kendrick leaned forward and rested his elbows on his knees. "Thank you. I had to change my outlook. Instead of being angry about her being taken away so young, I had to thank God for at least giving me twenty-six great years with her."

What should have felt awkward for Kaycee to talk about actually helped her to understand Kendrick better. She respected and admired that woman who had helped to build the faith of the man sitting beside her, and she found herself wanting to know more about him.

"Kendrick, do you mind me asking how old you are?"

He shrugged. "Forty-eight."

Her eyes bucked. "Wow,"

"What's that supposed to mean?" he asked.

"Nothing. It's just that I didn't think you were forty-eight. You look great."

"Thanks," he replied, pretending to brush dust from his sleeves with pride. He stopped to return the question.

With a hesitant smile, Kaycee revealed that she was twenty-nine.

"I figured you were around my daughter's age."

"Your daughter is twenty-nine?" she exclaimed in disbelief.

"Close, she's twenty-five."

"Wow," was all she could say.

"Do you have a problem with my age?" he asked.

"Like they say, age ain't nothing but a number," she answered, but that number—forty-eight—resonated in her head.

"Besides, I don't place limits on myself."

He picked up his plate and stabbed the salad with his fork.

"So, tell me your story, Kaycee. I know the young fella at Jireh that night has something to do with your past. Is he still someone to you?"

She gave him a sidelong glance. "Why do you say that?"

"I could tell by the way he had you all hemmed up," he retorted with a light chuckle. "He must have peed in his pants when I took you away. I can't stand when young brothers try to act like they own you females like that. Why do you all let them do that to you?"

Kaycee shrugged. "I don't know, I guess in some strange way it makes us feel like…like they really care about us."

He put his plate down and shook his head intently. He raised his finger, emphasizing his point.

"Any woman who's with me is going to know I care about her without me having to do anything like that."

His words were said with such conviction that they made her insides tingle.

"So, are you two still seeing each other?" he continued his questioning.

She shook her head. "Not at all. We broke up months ago."

"Why, may I ask?"

This time it was Kaycee's turn to spill her guts. "We had been dating for three years and weren't going anywhere. Just about the time I realized that I wasn't the woman I wanted to be with Paul, he proposed and I turned him down."

Kendrick quietly asked, "Did you have an identity problem or something?"

"No, but I thought I knew what I wanted. I thought I wanted the big house, fancy car, large income, but all of that doesn't even matter."

Kendrick eyed her skeptically, "Now, this house isn't small-time."

"But it's nothing compared to what I wanted," she quickly interjected. "We were looking at homes in the $600,000-plus range."

Kendrick whistled low. "Now, that's a lot of house."

"Tell me about it. But I came to my senses, purchased this home and the rest was history, including Paul."

"Wow, Ms. Jordan, you surprise me."

She held up her hand to stop him from going on. "First of all, do me a favor and drop the formalities if you don't mind. Kaycee is fine *all* the time."

Kendrick nodded in agreement.

"Okay, Kaycee," he repeated her name in a low, husky voice that she felt could paralyze her into submission.

She didn't know what it was that loomed between them, but it caught her off guard every time she was in his presence.

Both sighed with relief when the theme song of the movie began to play, providing a welcoming distraction.

Kaycee placed her plate in her lap and began to eat, masking the increasing hunger for another kind of nourishment that only Kendrick could provide.

Kaycee forgot how much Bond movies relaxed her. A good hour into the movie she had fallen asleep.

Three hours later, her eyes fluttered opened and adjusted to the only light in the room that emanated from the plasma television.

She was disappointed that she had fallen asleep and was equally surprised to find herself stretched out on the couch beside Kendrick.

Slowly, she eased from her spot so as not to awaken him and began to clear the table. Plates in hand, she stumbled into the kitchen where she learned that it was past midnight. After placing the plates in the sink, she put the remainder of the food in the refrigerator.

She returned to the family room and a slight smile curved her mouth at the sight of Kendrick sleeping in a sitting position with his head leaning back on the cushion.

He looked peaceful, as if he belonged there, bringing a sense of calm and security into her home. Kaycee tiptoed in closer to examine him without interruption. Her fascination extended beyond Kendrick's business expertise and knowledge. Mostly, it was the care and concern that he displayed for her well-being. Then there were the simple things, such as the way his brows knit together when he was deep in thought or how his smile was reminiscent of the radiant sun with all thirty-two pearlies gleaming bright just for her.

She slowly eased back down beside him.

Her eyes fell upon his succulent lips and she wondered how they would feel against her body.

She was inching closer, examining his handsome features, when the ringing of her cell phone startled them both. Kaycee sprang up from the sofa, her heart pounding in her chest. A barrage of questions rattled through her mind. What was she thinking, getting close to him like that? What if he woke up? Then what?

She stood off to the side, watching as he repositioned himself and seemed to go back to sleep. When the phone rang a second time, she snatched it off the coffee table.

"Hello?" she asked, watching Kendrick yawn. He leaned forward and stretched out his arms.

"Kaycee, I hope I'm not calling too late," a male voice said.

"Um—it's okay. Who is this?" she asked.

"This is Grant."

"Grant?" she repeated, then wished she hadn't as Kendrick looked up immediately at the mention of another man's name.

"Grant Craddock, Sidra's friend."

"Hello." Her eyes were on Kendrick, who was now sitting on the edge of the sofa.

"As I said, I hope I'm not calling at a bad time."

"It's not too late," she answered.

He exhaled in relief. "I'm glad. I really wanted to talk to you. Sidra speaks well of you."

"The same of you," she uttered.

Kendrick's mouth pulled to one side in annoyance.

"I was hoping we could meet for lunch."

Kaycee's eyes averted from Kendrick's face and she slightly turned. "That would be nice."

"Are you free tomorrow?"

She looked around as if she was searching for a calendar when she knew good and well there was none to be found.

"Tomorrow? I'm not sure. Let me check my calendar to be sure and I'll call you back tomorrow."

"Sure, I'll look forward to hearing from you."

"I'll let you know."

The line went dead.

Kaycee flipped the phone shut and tossed it on the table. She turned back to Kendrick with a smile as sweet as candy.

"Did you sleep well?"

Rather than answer her question, he looked around the room before resting his eyes on her again.

"What time is it?"

"A little after midnight," she answered.

He snorted with a shake of his head and stood. "Let me get out of your way."

Kaycee knew his sudden distance had something to do with Grant's call. She could have kicked herself for answering the phone and saying Grant's name. She followed closely behind as Kendrick sauntered through the kitchen and down the hall toward the front door.

"What time shall I report for work tomorrow?" she blurted out in an effort to delay him from walking through the door.

Kendrick paused for a moment, giving her hope, yet making her nervous at the same time.

Finally, he uttered, "Nine o'clock will be fine."

"Okay, I'll see you bright and early!" she called out with added cheer, hoping to alleviate the tension that had fallen between them. She wanted to say more but felt it wouldn't be appropriate, not at this stage. She watched as he undid the locks and opened the door.

"Good night, Ms. Jordan," he said without turning around.

The strides they'd made in getting to know one another better seemed futile, and Kaycee believed that they were back to square one.

"Damn," Kendrick muttered as he stepped into his kitchen through the garage. He felt stupid. Like a schoolboy hanging around outside the window of the cheerleading captain who didn't know or care that he was alive.

"What does she have on me?" he shouted out into the empty room, his voice resonating against the walls. The silence offered him no answers. Tossing his car keys on the kitchen counter, he headed straight for the wet bar in the sunken family room.

There, he pulled out a bottle of cognac. He twisted off the lid and poured a shot glass full. Raising the amber liquid to his mouth, he paused.

Never would he believe that a woman could make him drink, but Kaycee Jordan was doing all kinds of things to him that made him respond in strange ways. He closed his eyes.

Instantly he pictured himself carrying her in his arms beyond the tall mahogany doors to his master suite. Shaking his head to clear the picture, Kendrick swallowed down the contents of the glass, its heat burning past his esophagus and roaring in his chest.

Kaycee stirred emotions that had lain dormant since Amanda's passing, emotions that Kendrick had always believed belonged to his wife alone.

The possibility of opening himself to a woman again scared yet intrigued him. Kaycee's presence was energizing and made him look forward to each day in anticipation. Yet the mysterious phone call put a damper on everything. Who was this Grant person? he asked himself, his jaw tightening with jealous anger. The fact that another man could be in the picture drew forth a territorial spirit such as he had never known. Whoever Grant was, he had to get out of the picture because Kendrick himself had no plans of bowing out graciously.

Chapter 11

"What is mer-an-goo?" Charlotte asked, peering over the tops of her glasses at the sign-up sheet Kaycee was posting on the wall.

Kaycee giggled, "That's pronounced *mer-an-gay*, Charlotte, and it's a form of Latin dancing."

Charlotte frowned. "Okay, what does that have to do with Jireh?"

"It's a new marketing strategy that Mr. Thompson and I came up with to draw different clientele." She handed a poster to the older woman. "On the first Saturday of each month, we're going to have Latin dance lessons. You should come, you'll like it."

Charlotte snorted. "I don't know nothing about Latin anything, especially 'bout none of them dances."

Kaycee smiled. "Don't knock it till you try it, Charlotte. They say that Latin dancing is the body language of love, like speaking Spanish." She swayed her hips to an imaginary beat.

"Who said that?" Charlotte grumbled with a suck of her teeth and a roll of her eyes. "Can't nothing beat the Isley Brothers when it comes to the language of love."

"I know that's right!" Kaycee chimed in.

"What's right?"

Both women turned around to find Otis standing there with a smirk on his face.

"Oh, nobody's talking to you, Otis Sharpe, go on back in that kitchen!" Charlotte hollered.

"Cool off, woman," he bellowed. "I heard somebody say something about the Isley Brothers and love."

"And your point is?" Charlotte retorted with her hand on her hip.

"My point is that I know better than either one of you know about the Isley Brothers. I grew up with Ron Isley, you know."

"Yeah, right," Charlotte scoffed.

"I did," he insisted, pressing an indignant thumb against his chest. "We used to run the block together."

Charlotte rolled her eyes. "Anyway, why don't you run your little self back to that kitchen and get ready for lunch before the crowd gets in?"

Kaycee fell over in laughter watching the pair heckle each another like an old married couple. She couldn't help but wonder if there was something between them.

Their bantering was interrupted when the door opened. On cue, all playing was set aside and replaced with professionalism. Otis immediately headed back to the kitchen while Charlotte took to wiping off the counter.

"Welcome to Café…" Her words trailed off as an exotic-looking man sauntered through the entrance. He was about six feet tall with a handsome face and a slim but well-built body. It wasn't his curly Afro that caught Kaycee's attention, but rather the striking green eyes contrasting with his caramel skin and wide, pearly-white smile.

"Welcome to Café Jireh, how can we help you?"

He smiled, flashing a dimple in one cheek. "Hello, ladies, I'm looking for Kaycee Jordan."

"I'm Kaycee."

He beamed harder and held out his hand. "It's nice to finally meet you. I'm Grant Craddock, Sidra's friend."

"Oh, hi, Grant," she said, extending her hand. "It's nice to meet you, too."

"I hope you don't mind me coming by the place. I couldn't resist the urge, especially after Sidra told me you work here." He gazed around. "I've heard so many good things about it."

Kaycee nodded. She didn't know what to make of him coming to her job, but then, she knew when Sidra had something up her sleeve.

"Thank you, it's a great place," Kaycee said. The three of them stood there smiling awkwardly until Charlotte cleared her throat.

"Where are my manners?" Kaycee said, and quickly introduced the two.

"My, my, my, are those your eyes?" Charlotte blurted out as if she couldn't wait to ask. She moved closer.

Grant blushed. "Yes ma'am. Got them from my daddy."

"Are you that guy off the movie *Barbershop?*"

Grant laughed. He was used to the attention he received from people—especially ladies—over his resemblance to actor Michael Ealy. "No ma'am, I actually work in investments."

"I'll invest in it, whatever it is," Charlotte said with a low whistle. She winked at Kaycee before reclaiming her post behind the counter.

"I'll remember that." He turned back to Kaycee. "I'm sorry, I should have called to see if it was okay to come."

"No, no, no, you're fine," she assured him. "I can use a short break anyway." She picked up a menu and two sets of flatware.

She led him toward the back of the dining room

to a secluded booth by the window with a view of the back patio.

"Is this good?"

"Perfect," he replied, sliding in while Kaycee sat opposite him.

Once they were settled in, Kaycee handed him the menu.

Grant opened it up, his eyes scanning the offerings. "Tell me what's good."

"Everything," she replied. "And I'm not just saying that. Otis, the head chef, is an excellent cook." She was glad that she had made up a fresh batch of desserts the night before. Kaycee waved for Charlotte to come over and take their order.

"You two ready to order?" Charlotte said and placed two glasses of water before them.

"Although everything looks tempting, I'm not very hungry, so I think I'll just have a chai latte for now," Grant announced.

"Sounds good to me," Kaycee added. "I'll have the same, Charlotte."

Charlotte retrieved the menus and departed, leaving Kaycee and Grant sitting together with nervous smiles on their faces. It was Grant who broke the ice.

"You know, when Sidra said she had a friend for me to meet, I was hesitant, but I'm glad I set aside my reservations."

"I don't know if that's a compliment or not."

"Trust me, it is," he quickly replied.

Kaycee was too preoccupied to be flattered by Grant's compliment. Every once in a while she would peer over his shoulder for signs of Kendrick, even though he wasn't scheduled to return for two hours.

She hoped to visit with Grant and have him out of the building way before Kendrick's return, though she didn't know why it mattered, since he had gone back to his ice-cold self after that night at her home.

While Grant talked, her thoughts strayed to Kendrick. He attracted her on many levels. He had charisma. He was generous and had a calmness about him that was infectious. She couldn't deny that he was also fine!

But, there were so many odds against them even being together. For one, Kendrick was a man who hadn't completely gotten over the loss of his beloved wife. He was old enough to be her father. He happened to have a daughter her age, and she clearly remembered his comment about not being interested in distractions.

"Tell me about yourself, Kaycee," Grant said, interrupting her thoughts of Kendrick.

Kaycee quickly took a sip of water as she wondered where she should start. "There's not much to tell. I'm from Atlanta, although people swear that I'm not because I don't have a Southern accent."

"An original Georgia peach?"

"That's right," she replied.

"Did you go to school here?"

She nodded, "University of Georgia."

"Bulldog, huh?"

"All the way. From there I went straight into corporate America like every other ambitious graduate, only to learn it wasn't for me."

She paused when Charlotte arrived with their drinks.

Grant waited until Charlotte departed before speaking again. "Why wasn't the corporate thing for you?"

"I felt like I was losing myself."

"How so?" he asked, raising the mug to his lips.

"I didn't like where I was in my life. The whole corporate thing wasn't me. I felt I was living a facade that did not represent who I was inside. I always wanted to own my own business so I stepped out and started Soulicious Gourmet Desserts and Event Planning."

"Just like that?"

She snapped her fingers. "Just like that."

"Impressive," he said shaking his head. "How did you hook up with Jireh?"

Bringing Kendrick into their conversation made Kaycee very uneasy. For the first time since Grant's arrival, she felt almost as if she were betraying him by entertaining another man on his premises.

"Actually, the owner is my neighbor. He's a really nice guy," she responded vaguely.

"Wow, talk about being in the right place at the right time."

Kaycee nodded and took another sip of her drink. "What about you, Grant? Sidra said you're an engineer."

He nodded, "I build houses. I have some subdivisions I'm working on now." He rattled off a few in nearby communities.

"Do you live in any of the houses you build?" she asked.

He sat back against the seat and sighed. "You know, I have plans for my dream home, but I'm holding off on them until I get married."

"Why?" Kaycee asked. "If it's your dream, why not live it now?"

He shrugged. "I guess I just want my wife to feel like it's something we're doing together as a couple."

"How sweet," Kaycee gushed.

Grant smiled with relief at her simple compliment.

They talked for a while longer, sharing their likes and dislikes, their travels and favorite pastimes until Grant looked at his watch. His eyes widened in surprise.

"You know, I'm enjoying this visit very much, but I really have to get back to the office."

"I understand, I have to get back to work myself," she replied, standing.

They walked to the entrance together.

"May I call you again? Maybe plan something later in the evening when we have more time?"

"Sure." Kaycee decided that their conversation had been good. Grant seemed nice. She didn't have the somersaulting feeling she had when Kendrick was near, but that was okay. Grant was easygoing and, for Kaycee, very safe.

"I will give you a call," Grant said holding out his hand for her to shake.

Kaycee placed her hand in his and was surprised by its softness. The man definitely did not know hard labor. "Sounds good. Thanks for stopping by."

He leaned down and placed a friendly kiss on Kaycee's cheek. She was so completely thrown off guard by his action that she didn't see Kendrick walking into the door.

Kendrick came to a quick halt right before the couple. His eyes went from Kaycee to Grant to his lips on her cheek and they narrowed. He cleared his throat loudly.

Kaycee jumped then groaned inwardly at the sight of Kendrick standing there. She immediately stepped back from Grant.

"Kendri—I mean, Mr. Thompson," she stammered.

Kendrick's brow raised at her formality, but he said nothing.

"Grant, allow me to introduce you to the owner of

Café Jireh, Kendrick Thompson. Kendrick Thompson, Grant Craddock." After making introductions, Kaycee stepped back, wishing that she could melt into the floor.

Grant held out his hand. "This man needs no introduction! Kendrick Thompson, safety for the Pittsburgh Steelers. It's a pleasure meeting you!"

When Kendrick failed to acknowledge him, he continued rambling. "Man, wait until I tell my boys, they won't believe it. Hey, I really like what you've done to the place. It's tight, man." He whipped out a business card. "I'm on the board of the Black Business Network. Let me know if there's anything I can do to throw some business your way."

Kendrick muttered a quick thanks before turning his attention onto Kaycee. His eyes were full of accusation laced with disappointment.

"Ms. Jordan, when you are done fraternizing with the customers, I need to see you in my office." He announced before turning and walking away.

Heat rose up her neck as she watched Kendrick stalk away without a care to how he made her look. "Grant, I'm sorry. Duty calls. I will talk with you later."

"I hope I didn't cause any trouble."

Kaycee shook her head with a forced smile. "You're fine."

"I'll call you," he said before hurrying out the door.

Upon Grant's exit, Kaycee frowned and slowly

turned her head in the direction that Kendrick had headed. How dare he try to embarrass her like that! They were business associates, nothing more. She was not his employee nor was she his child, and she wasn't about to be treated as such.

Ignoring the look of surprise on Charlotte's face, she stomped back to Kendrick's office.

Kendrick was sitting in his chair staring at the wall when Kaycee stormed into the office.

She slammed her palms on the desk in front of him. "What was that all about?" she cried.

"Ms. Jordan, please close the door," he calmly replied.

Kaycee turned swiftly and slammed the door, causing the calendar on the back to swing back and forth like a pendulum. Her action made Kendrick sit up at full attention.

"Satisfied?" she curtly asked.

"Very," he answered, easing back in his chair with his palms resting behind his head.

Kaycee rolled her eyes. "I'm glad one of us is." She stood up and paced before his desk. "Kendrick, what is this all about?"

He didn't answer her right away. His thoughts were consumed by her dark delicate image. Although her eyes flashed like lightning, he imagined himself calming the storm within with a gentle stroke of his hand. He hated that he had to get her attention in that manner, but it was all he could do short of knocking old pretty boy to the floor. He'd resolved the other night that his attraction to her was more than a fleeting passion, but fondness and kinship.

"I don't like the way you were carrying on with the customer like that. It was unprofessional."

Her brow furrowed. "What are you talking about?"

He half laughed with a shake of his head. "Come on, Kaycee, the kiss on the cheek."

"I didn't know he was going to do that!" she cried out.

"Well, I don't want to see that kind of thing out there like that in front of our customers." Or me, he added in his head.

"Kendrick, it wasn't like I asked him to do it. You just happened to walk in. What was I supposed to do? Push him away?"

"That would have been a start," he quickly replied, then turned away, hating himself for displaying his feelings about the situation. His words brought to light the truth of the matter.

A slight smile curved her lips as she recognized his behavior. "Well, excuse me, but I didn't know you cared."

"I—I don't," he stuttered nervously. He didn't want Kaycee to read what he was truly feeling, so he began to shuffle through some papers on his desk. "I just thought it wasn't appropriate."

Kaycee threw her arms up in the air and plopped down in a nearby chair. "Kendrick, are you really that uptight?"

His head whipped in her direction. Was it showing?

"What? Me uptight? Please, I'm the most relaxed person you'll ever know."

"I don't know," she chided. "Since I've met you, it's like being in a tornado. One minute you seem like you're up, then the next minute, you're down. I don't know who I'm going to get on a given day. Don't you know how to relax?"

When he was around Kaycee, there was hardly such a word as *relax,* especially not when all he wanted to do was pull her into his arms. He guessed that relaxation would come only after he'd had the opportunity to taste her luscious mouth. "Yes, I know how to relax."

"I think you have the potential, but you're—you're too uptight."

"I'm not uptight. Just because I don't think it's appropriate for a man to be all over a woman in public doesn't mean I'm uptight."

Kaycee giggled. "Okay, tell me, what do you do to relax then?" she challenged.

Kendrick turned away so she could not see his first choice reflected in his eyes. He forced his mind toward purer thoughts, such as the things that he really enjoyed doing. He was an outdoors man and appreciated fishing when he had the time.

"I like to fish."

Kaycee's eyes widened. "No, you don't."

"Why wouldn't I?" he asked. "Fishing is a great stress reliever for me."

"I love to fish, too," she said in awe. He immediately wondered what was happening. First James Bond and now fishing. The idea of the two of them sharing another passion was making it hard for his body to agree with his head. Everything about Kaycee seemed so right for him.

"You? I have to see it to believe it!"

"Hey, I'm good," Kaycee exclaimed with her chin poked out confidently.

His eyes narrowed with skepticism. "What's your biggest catch?"

"A twenty-four-inch-long widemouth bass. I caught it on a fishing trip with my dad in south Georgia."

"You fish with your father?"

She nodded. "All the time, although I haven't lately. See, we have an annual father-daughter fishing trip, but I had to cancel last year."

"Why's that?"

"With the move and the new business, I couldn't work it into my schedule," she answered. She sighed in disappointment. "My dad and I have had some good times. He always made sure to make our trip special. He'd pack my sleeping bag and air mattress, books, magazines, radio and my favorite snacks—Pepsi, Doritos and peanut M&Ms—everything to make our trip perfect."

"You're a daddy's girl?" Kendrick asked, engaged in her reminiscences.

She nodded. "I'm his *only* girl."

Kendrick chuckled. "I don't know if I can see you roughing it in the woods, especially with those high heels you wear."

Kaycee rolled her eyes. "I'm always a lady, but I know when to fold 'em and when to hold 'em."

"I've got to see this. I'm rolling out of here on Saturday morning at 3:00 a.m. Are you with me?"

Kaycee's eyes lit up her face and twinkled mischievously. "Are you sure you can handle this?"

"Very sure," he replied.

Nodding her head in confirmation, she rose from her seat and headed for the door.

"Oh, Kaycee, one more thing. I rough it. That means no electricity or running water, I hope that won't ruin it for you."

"I'm not the one to worry about," she coolly replied.

Her response led Kendrick to believe that she was probably right.

Chapter 12

"You're going where?" Sidra exclaimed in disbelief as she followed Kaycee from the family room to the garage where Kaycee began her search for her small cooler.

"I'm going camping with Kendrick," she replied as she pulled a tarp from atop the boxes stacked in the corner. She spotted the red cooler sitting back against the wall.

"A camping trip with Kendrick? Kaycee, have you lost your mind?"

"Nope," she replied as she began moving the

boxes out of the way. They were heavy. She wondered what was inside them.

"Grant told me that he invited you to the Anthony Hamilton concert and you turned him down because you said you had plans."

"That's right," Kaycee sang as she pulled the cooler from its spot.

Sidra exhaled loudly. "And your plans include a fishing trip?"

"Uh-huh," Kaycee confirmed with a preoccupied nod.

"Kaycee, are you crazy?"

Kaycee looked at Sidra and giggled. "Maybe I am."

Sidra took the cooler from Kaycee's hands and set it on the garage floor.

"Can I have your attention please!"

Kaycee sucked her teeth and cocked her head to the side, annoyed by Sidra's interruptions. "Sidra, what is it?"

She had exactly one hour to finish packing and get into bed so that she could rise early in the morning.

"I'll tell you what it is. You are making a fool of yourself by getting involved with that man."

Kaycee looked at Sidra as though she wanted to slap her. "What are you talking about?" she asked. She picked up the cooler and headed back inside the house.

"He's your neighbor, he's your boss and most important—he's old enough to be your daddy! What are you gaining by involving yourself with him?"

Kaycee placed the cooler on the counter and spun around in anger. "For your information, Sidra, Kendrick and I are not involved, we are just friends. Furthermore, if I choose to take it to another level, it's no one's business but mine."

Sidra sighed. "I'm just looking out for you, girl."

"I'm a grown woman."

"You're also a woman who already lost a good portion of her life on a man who wasn't worth two dead flies. Thank God you got a revelation and let him go. I just don't want to see you make the same mistake that you made with Paul."

Kaycee inhaled deeply and closed her eyes before exhaling slowly through her mouth.

"Thank you for your advice, Sidra, but I know what I'm doing."

Sidra picked up her purse, "Kayce, don't be mad at me. I'm just looking out for your best interests."

"Oh, really? Since you know so much, what are my best interests?"

"I know you want to be married. I know you want kids. Is he willing to give you those things?"

Kaycee rolled her eyes in irritation. "Listen Sid, Kendrick is a very nice man. I really enjoy his company and I'm going on this fishing trip. I'm not trying to marry him and I'm not trying to bear his children. He asked me to go and I accepted. You know I love to fish." She began to push Sidra to the front door. "Now, I appreciate your concerns, but I am a big girl."

Sidra dug her feet into the floor long enough to say, "I hope so," before stumbling out.

Kaycee groaned as the door closed behind her. She neither needed nor wanted Sidra's advice about Kendrick.

She hoped she hadn't made a mistake telling her friend about the trip. After all, she and Kendrick had decided to keep it from the staff at Jireh. Although the trip was innocent, they didn't want there to be any talk. As far as the staff knew, Kendrick was going fishing alone and Kaycee was taking a couple of days off.

There was definitely something special between the two of them, and it was so good that she wasn't about to let any social mores or personal opinions sabotage it.

Kaycee's cell phone rang at exactly four o'clock. She was up, sitting at the island in her kitchen and drinking a cup of coffee.

"Hello."

"Are you ready?" Kendrick's smooth voice asked, causing Kaycee to smile.

"Ready and waiting on you," she replied. "I got coffee, would you like a cup?"

"Oh, so you're in the coffee business now?" he joked. "I guess you have learned some things since you've been at Jireh after all."

"Ha, ha. Come on in, the garage door is up."

For the trip, Kaycee had selected a practical yet comfortable outfit: sporty khaki capri pants, her favorite orange polo shirt and a pair of matching sneakers. Kendrick surprised her by arriving dressed in similar attire: khaki painter-style jeans, orange T-shirt and boots. There was no way that anyone could tell that the man was a day over thirty-five.

"You got the memo," he teased, entering through the door to the garage and spotting her outfit.

Kaycee laughed along with him, and snuck an appreciative glance as he reached for her bag.

He turned around quickly, catching her in the act of watching him.

"Now, Ms. Jordan, I know you aren't trying to flatter me."

"Kendrick!" she cried out with embarrassment. "Even if I was, you didn't have to say anything."

He laughed as he said, "Kaycee, I like seeing you get all embarrassed."

"Why?" she asked.

"Because it shows that you're human," he replied evenly, flicking a curled finger gently beneath her chin.

Excitement fluttered in her stomach as she grabbed

the cups of coffee that she had poured into traveling mugs and followed him.

The engine on Kendrick's black truck hummed softly in the darkness. He pressed the button unlocking the doors and the pair walked to the back to load her things. Kaycee spotted portable lounge chairs, a boom box, a case of CDs ranging from R&B to neo-soul to jazz-and-blues, and a bag containing a six-pack of Pepsi, a large bag of Doritos and peanut M&Ms.

"Kendrick, what are these for?" she asked.

"For you," he solemnly replied as he maneuvered things around to make room for her bags.

"Y-you did this for me?" she asked. She didn't know what to make of his gesture. It was acts of kindness such as this that warmed her heart and restored her faith in the man.

"Yes," he replied without looking at her. "I wanted your trip to be comfortable."

"Thank you," she said touched by his thoughtfulness. "I appreciate it."

At the sound of the shakiness in her voice, he spun around and gazed into her eyes. "You're welcome."

No other words were exchanged as they put all of her things inside and went around to get in their seats.

As Kendrick backed out of the driveway and onto the road, Kaycee thought of the chemistry between them. It was heavy, filled with fire and connection. She couldn't understand how one minute she loathed him and the next minute she wanted him. Finally, an inkling of understanding crept into her consciousness, making her wonder if they were strong enough to return from this trip the same way that they left.

They drove nearly three hours out of the city to a quiet rural community that was just waking. Kaycee could see the signs of life as they passed the lit-up truck stop and local café. Kendrick drove through the town and on for about five minutes before turning off onto a gravel road.

The truck bounced and jiggled on the uneven road and Kaycee hoped that this was no indication of what was to come. The first thing that came to mind was the Beverly Hillbillies before they went Beverly Hills.

Although she was the outdoors type, she wasn't as rustic as she'd made Kendrick believe. She was still female and desired the luxuries synonymous with being one.

About a mile along the gravel road, Kendrick made a turn onto a road that was lined with dense trees. Kaycee was immediately reminded of the out-of-the-way campsites featured in the scary movie *Friday the 13th*. *Deliverance* also came to mind. After all, they were in the north Georgia mountains! The thought of being dragged away by a psychopathic hillbilly made her shudder.

Kendrick must have picked up on her mounting fears because he reached over and grabbed her hand.

"It's not so bad," he assured her. "I know this area like the back of my hand. I know many of the towns-people, as well. You have nothing to be afraid of."

His ability to read her emotions was enough to make her relax.

The cabin was set in the middle of a clearing. It was a new cabin designed to look antiquated, with its open porch and wooden swing. However, the grass was somewhat overgrown, as if no one had inhabited the place in some time.

"I know it doesn't look like a palace," Kendrick began, "but believe me, the inside will change your mind."

He jumped out of the truck and cursed as he realized how high the foliage had grown, reaching almost as high as his knees. "That damn Jack knew I was coming out today," he said, shaking his head in disbelief. "He could have had the decency to cut the grass before he left."

"Who's Jack?" Kaycee asked from her seat in the car. She was still trying to gather up enough nerve to get out.

"A friend. We both own this cabin. He was up a couple of weeks ago and knew that I was coming up this weekend. He promised me that he would cut the grass."

"Oh," was all Kaycee could reply, while hoping and praying that Kendrick had been pulling her leg about the amenities and that there was hot running water inside.

Kendrick went around the back of the truck and began to remove the contents.

"Should you check the inside first?" Kaycee called out uneasily from the front seat.

"It's fine," he answered in return. He slipped his bag on one shoulder and hers on the other, placed the folding chairs under his arms and the coolers in his hands and headed up the cobbled walk.

"Wait here and I'll be right back," he instructed.

"You don't have to tell me twice," she answered with a shudder.

When he unlocked and opened the door, she leaned forward to see if he would be met by a tangle of cobwebs attached to a big hairy spider or two; she was surprised there was none.

She sat and waited and waited for him to return to give her the okay. About fifteen minutes passed before she got tired of waiting. She said a prayer for protection, grabbed her purse and stepped out.

She tiptoed through the grass, trying to avoid an encounter with a sleeping snake. When she reached the walk, she ran the rest of the way until she was on the porch.

She stood there for a few seconds mentally preparing herself for the most simplistic living experience. Her experience in summer camp came to mind.

Creaky floors, hard thin mattresses on hard beds, a fireplace for a stove and heat source and a pump at the sink. And as for indoor plumbing— forget it. The Moon, as it was called, was fifty yards out back.

However, when she crossed the cabin's threshold, she was surprised to feel as though she had stepped right into a home decor magazine. She could see that her fears could be put to rest. The room screamed "decorator" from its hand-carved knickknacks to the faux bear head mounted on the wall.

The colors of red, brown and cream covering the chairs and sofa in different patterns and textures added a sophisticated flair. What caught her eye immediately was the ten-foot-high limestone fireplace with an opening tall enough for an adult to walk into.

"Kendrick!" she called out his name.

When the toilet flushed in response, she raised her hands to the heavens—thank you Lord! Running water!

He stepped out of the bathroom drying his hands on a towel.

"Does the place meet your expectations?"

"Does it!" she exclaimed, looking around at the comfortable decor. "This is very nice!"

"Thank you," he replied. "I put your things in the bedroom straight back."

Kaycee turned to see the lone door at the end of the hallway. Although cozy and fashionably decorated, the cabin was small with only one bedroom and one bathroom.

"Where are you going to sleep?" she asked out of curiosity.

He patted the couch. "It sleeps very well."

She shook her head. "I can't do that. I can't put you out."

"It's okay. Besides, I need to be out here to protect you."

"Protect me from what?"

"Lions, tigers or bears."

Kaycee laughed. "Anyway."

"Seriously, I would rather be out here. I put your things in the bedroom. Now, let's get to the lake before the fish decide to sleep in."

Grabbing her wide-brimmed straw hat, Kaycee jumped to it and helped to put the remainder of the things away. Finally, with tackle boxes, folding chairs and rods in hand, the pair scampered down the hill to the picturesque lake below. The view was magnificent, and Kaycee stopped frequently to take it all in.

The lake was surrounded by trees and meadows that were scattered with colorful wildflowers. At its edge was a wooden pier. A tire swing hanging from one of the trees brought Norman Rockwell paintings to mind.

"Kendrick, this is beautiful!" Kaycee breathed.

He turned with a thoughtful smile. "I thought you would like it." He reached for her hand and led her down the rest of the path and onto the pier.

Kendrick handed Kaycee the fishing rods as he set up everything. Kaycee was too awestruck to help. The clean air filled her nose and she inhaled deeply, cleansing her lungs.

The sound of birds singing and crickets chirping was beautiful music to her ears.

"This is so amazing," she said in awe. "You know, all my life, I thought I was a city girl, but I seriously think I could live out here."

"Could you really?" Kendrick asked with his head cocked to the side in disbelief.

She nodded, gazing around. "It's so beautiful."

As they both stood taking in the sights and sounds, a pair of deer broke through the brush on the opposite side of the lake. Kaycee held her breath as they timidly stepped down to the edge of the lake for a drink.

"Oh, look," she cooed softly.

"Shh," he whispered, leading her over to the chairs that he'd set up.

Kaycee eased down in the chair and removed her jacket. Kendrick did the same. As they watched the life around them awaken, they totally forgot about fishing.

About an hour later, the darkness gave way to the light and it was time to do what they came for.

Kendrick took Kaycee's rod to prepare the line, but she took it from his hands.

"Kendrick, I'm not a wimpy girl. I know how to do this," she scolded him.

He let it go without a word and watched as she swung the rod back and whipped it quickly forward, sending it deep into the center of the lake.

"Good job!" he exhorted.

She did a little shoulder dance, picked up her soda and eased back into her seat.

Simultaneously, they both lowered their hats onto their heads and waited.

In a matter of hours, the temperatures had climbed to a sweltering ninety degrees. Kendrick leaned over the bucket between them and looked down at the dozen or so fish flopping in the shallow water.

"It's getting kind of hot," he announced peering up into the sky. "I think we should call it quits. We did pretty good, don't you think?"

"We?" Kaycee asked. "Most of those are mine."

Kendrick laughed. "Okay, I'll give it to you. You know what you're doing."

"Thank you," she replied. "That's all I needed to hear." She sat up and wiped her forehead with the back of her hand. She picked up the bucket and started for the edge of the pier.

He jumped up and grabbed her by the wrist.

"Where are you going with those?"

"Tossing them back in," she casually replied. She lifted the bucket only to be stopped by his hand once more.

"Why would you do that?"

"Didn't I tell you that I don't eat the fish that I catch?"

He frowned. "You don't eat the fish you catch? What kind of mess is that?"

She shrugged. "I can't make myself do it."

"Well, you're fine to throw your fish back, but I will be eating mine," he said taking the bucket from her.

"You talking about those three little trout?" she teased. "Because you know the majority of them are mine."

"Ha, ha. I bet you'll be begging for some of that trout tonight when I fry it up."

"Let's hope that's all I'll be begging for," she mumbled.

"What did you say?" he asked with a raised brow.

Kaycee stilled as heat radiated up her neck and onto her face. She hoped he hadn't heard her comment. "Nothing."

Kendrick shrugged and picked up the bucket and fishing poles.

"I'll show you around before we go back to the cabin."

"Cool," she said, liking the idea of exploring her surroundings.

It didn't take them long to cover the premises. As they walked along, Kendrick explained how the trees and brush were strategically placed to give the cabin more of a private, out-of-the-way feel.

There was a storage barn where he kept ATVs and yard equipment, and a man-made gravel trail took them all the way around the lake and up a hill where there was a combination hunting stand and treehouse complete with a step ladder and rope.

"Would you like to go up and see the view?" he asked.

"Sure," she replied.

Kendrick allowed her to climb first. When she got a third of the way up he followed. Once Kaycee got to the top, Kendrick had to shimmy up behind her to push open the trapdoor. He was so close to her that he could smell the fresh scent of her hair lotion and feel her shiver from his closeness. Although his position was innocent, it was intimate all the same.

The platform of the treehouse provided a gorgeous view of the mountains to the north.

"I wish I had a camera," Kaycee said in a breath-less voice.

"Every time I come up here it always seems dif-ferent," he said.

They stood there for a little while, enjoying the

sounds of nature and the comfortable silence between them. Kaycee felt as though she could have stayed up there forever, and it was Kendrick who made the first move to go back. This time, however, he took the rope on the way down and challenged Kaycee to do the same, which she did like a champ.

By the time they returned from their walk it was almost noon and both of them were starving.

The first place Kaycee headed was the shower. As she washed the grime off her body, she thought about how amazing the day had been. Although it could be classified a date, it wasn't like any other time she'd ever had with a man. Closing her eyes, she wiped the soapy washcloth over her breasts and imagined that it was Kendrick's hand. The fleeting thought sent her imagination soaring.

Although she shouldn't have gone there, Kaycee imagined Kendrick would be a skillful lover—a man with a slow hand like the Pointer Sisters sang about.

Like any other red-blooded, American, twenty-something woman, Kaycee loved a good man. She might be celibate, but she wasn't blind. However, she had standards, high standards, and she didn't even entertain the thought of being with a man unless they were in a strong, committed relationship. What messed her up was that those standards she set had gone right out the window the day she'd met Kendrick. She'd been trying to get back on that wagon ever since.

She was grateful for the cool water pelting her skin, keeping the heat on her flesh at bay. After she was scrubbed clean, Kaycee slathered on her lotion and slipped into a white tank top, denim shorts and a pair of flip-flops. She finger-combed her hair with some moisturizer and left it to air-dry.

When she exited the bathroom, Kendrick was sitting in the chair facing the door. He nodded with appreciation.

"What's that supposed to mean?" she asked with a raised brow.

"You look nice," he stated directly.

His straightforward response made Kaycee blush, and she quickly made a beeline for the kitchen.

While Kendrick took his turn in the shower, Kaycee got their lunch together. She pulled out her cooler and began to remove different kinds of deli meats and cheeses, rye and sourdough bread, a container of deviled eggs, a small fruit tray containing strawberries, raspberries, mango and green grapes and a vegetable tray with pickles, green olives, carrots and celery. Add in the items Kendrick had brought and Kaycee was sure they would have a feast.

When the shower turned off, Kaycee turned to the sink to wash the dishes she'd found in the cupboard. After a few minutes, the door creaked open.

"What kind of meat would you like?" she called out without turning around.

Kendrick leaned his back against the door, his eyes watching Kaycee's bottom wiggling back and forth from the action of washing the dishes. Seeing Kaycee in his kitchen made him realize that it had been a long time since he'd desired female companionship.

"Kendrick?" she repeated and peered over her shoulder. Her mouth gaped open at him standing there wearing nothing more than a pair of jogging pants. Like the first day she met him, Kaycee was mesmerized by his bare beauty. In her eyes, God had created the perfect form when he made man, especially Kendrick.

Their eyes locked for a moment as if sending lewd mental text messages. It was Kendrick who broke the silence.

"Did you say something?"

She paused and looked to the sky for the answer. The heat she'd felt brewing in her abdomen earlier had returned in full force and she was getting weak.

"I—I—I'm making sandwiches," she stuttered. "Wh-what kind of meat would you like?"

"I'll take turkey," he answered as he sauntered across the room and picked up his duffel. If she only knew.

He pulled out a T-shirt and slipped it over his head, then joined her at the island in the middle of the room. His eyes brightened at the spread before him.

"Looks good," he commented and plopped down on a nearby stool.

Kaycee doled a little of everything onto both of their plates. She watched as Kendrick bit into his man-sized sandwich and rolled his eyes back in his head.

"This is good!" he groaned with satisfaction.

She smiled from behind her glass. She was glad to be able to do something special for him, even something as simple as preparing his lunch.

"Oh, I forgot something," he said, picking up his plate and soda. He beckoned for her to follow him.

Setting his food on the wooden trunk that doubled as a coffee table, Kendrick reached for his bag again. He fumbled around inside for a moment before producing his prize.

"Ta-da!" he said, holding up two James Bond DVDs.

"Now you're talking!" she blurted out and joined him on the sofa. He put in Kaycee's favorite, *Goldfinger*.

They settled down on the comfortable sofa, and no more than an hour into the movie they both fell fast asleep.

Chapter 13

The James Bond theme song repeated itself again and again, and Kaycee heard it in her subconscious, but it didn't register until it had played almost a dozen times.

Without opening her eyes, she stretched and shivered in the cool room; her body felt heat generating nearby. She gravitated toward it and snuggled against the warm solid mass.

A heavy arm fell over her waist with a hand that cupped her rear and her eyes quickly blinked awake. In the dimly lit room, she made out Kendrick's sleeping features.

"Kendrick," she whispered.

He stirred but did not wake.

She reached up and tapped him lightly on the chest, but all he did in response was inhale deeply, then exhale while pulling her closer in his embrace.

Kaycee smiled. She liked the feel of being in his arms. Their bodies lined up in every way, complementing and fitting.

Everything was right—the two of them, the setting—right for her to do what she'd had in her heart to do since their meeting. Kaycee stretched up so that she was face-to-face with Kendrick, and in slow motion she moved closer until their lips met. She gently brushed her mouth against his. The flames of need that she had been suppressing swelled into an outright inferno.

Kendrick's eyes sprang open, shocking her. The look in his eyes was more one of expectation than of surprise. He placed his hand on the back of Kaycee's neck and stroked her soft curls before pulling her back to his waiting mouth. His tongue parted her lips and plunged into her sweet recesses with fervor. He groaned through hungry kisses.

It wasn't enough to have her lying there beside him. Kendrick knew he needed her—desired her to be closer to him. He caught her off guard when he pulled her on top of him so that their bodies lined up perfectly. Where she curved he fit her like a glove, confirming again that they were meant to be.

They shared deep, passionate and ravenous kisses full of need, moving quickly from one motion to the next, stroking and tasting—fulfilling the fantasies that had played in their minds since that fateful day they'd met.

With a groan, Kendrick smoothed his hands down her back before sliding them lower onto the swell of her bottom and squeezing.

Kaycee moaned in response and swiveled her hips provocatively against him, causing his flesh to harden beneath her.

Her action stepped up the inferno to an explosion. Kendrick knew if he didn't stop, there would be no turning back. He gently took Kaycee's arms and pulled her up so that they were both in a seated position.

He cupped his hand lovingly against her cheek and gazed at her with admiring eyes. Kaycee's lashes fluttered under his intimate inspection.

Kendrick looked at her kiss-swollen lips and heaving breasts; he wanted to lay her down and make love—good love—to her all night long, but that wasn't his style. He wasn't a careless lover, nor was he thoughtless. He wanted to make sure that it was right.

"I want you," he admitted in a low, raspy whisper, stroking the softness of her cheek.

"I want you, too," she echoed. She turned her head slightly and kissed the center of his hand.

He cleared his throat. "But I want it to be right.

I'm not the kind of man who goes into these situations without a clear head."

"Okay," she breathed softly. She didn't know where he was going with this line, but she knew that she wanted him to ease the throbbing within her.

"I think we both need to think about what we are getting into and how we are going to handle this."

"What do you mean?" she asked. All he had to do was say the word and she would be all over him like white on rice, but the way he paused told her it wouldn't be that kind of evening.

"Kaycee, we have a lot to consider before we go there."

"What do we need to consider, Kendrick?" she purred.

He stood from his place on the sofa and walked across the room before turning around. "For starters, we work together, then there's the difference in our ages. I want to lay things out on the table upfront."

Kaycee smiled and said, "I'm aware of all that, Kendrick, and I still want to be with you. We're good together."

"Is that enough?" he asked.

She paused, then murmured, "I don't know, but I guess I'm willing to find out."

"Kaycee, I think we need to take things slow."

With a disappointed groan she moved away from him.

"Whoa, hear me out," he said, gently pulling her back. "There's no doubt that we are attracted to one another, and we are definitely compatible, but I think we need to really consider whether this is something that we want."

His announcement came as a disappointment.

"So, what are you suggesting?"

He paused. "I say we give each other space to think and look at the larger picture before we move on to the next level."

Kaycee couldn't believe her ears. Here she was alone with the man who had occupied her dreams, and he was talking about space.

"You don't want to see me anymore?" she squeaked.

Sensing her sadness, he pulled her into another embrace. The last thing he wanted to do was hurt her, but he knew that the right thing was to stop what they were doing before she got hurt further down the line. He brushed his lips against hers.

"I'm not saying that I don't want to see you, I—we need to make sure that this is a step that we both want to take."

Enveloped in the safety net of his embrace, Kaycee closed her eyes and nodded against his sturdy chest. She didn't know why he was doing this; she only hoped that this wasn't what would hurt them.

Chapter 14

Kendrick hesitated before stripping off his clothes following the intense workout he'd just had with his personal trainer. The workout was exhilarating and it showed in the sweat pouring down his face.

He couldn't wait to kick off the wet T-shirt and shorts and step into his three-headed shower and then into the sauna. He could almost picture himself languishing in the relaxing warmth.

He needed to relax. The last few months had him spinning. Most people would think such tension was natural with a business less than a year old, however, his anxiety had nothing to do with Café

Jireh, and everything to do with the brown-eyed girl next door.

Three days had passed since he had escorted her to her front door following their fishing trip, and with Tiki back home with Bianca, Kendrick didn't have to worry about anyone but himself. Being alone made him think about his aloneness.

As he walked down the hall to the bathroom, he passed the big portrait of Amanda and paused. Amanda had known him, loved him unconditionally and stood by him during his roughest times. If only he could have been as faithful.

She had shown him so much love. The affair during his football career had been forgiven. When he'd injured his knee during a preseason game and ended his career, she'd encouraged him to pursue other endeavors. When one night he'd felt that he wanted to end his life because of the void that weighed heavily in his heart, she'd introduced him to the peace and love that only a relationship with the Father could give.

Seven years following her death he still felt a sense of loyalty to his wife. There was a sense of comfort with her memory. However, he couldn't deny that Kaycee had a lot more in common with him than Amanda had had, which made it impossible to ignore the pull she had on him. His attentions and affections were being taken up by the young woman, and he felt guilty.

With a sigh, he took off his clothing and tossed

it in the laundry bin before heading straight for a cold shower.

Kendrick arrived at work late in the morning. The place was already filling up with the lunch crowd along with the regulars who spent the day tapping feverishly into their laptops.

His eyes scanned the dining room, and he was grateful to not see the familiar curly brown hair. Instead he found La Jetta and Jaylen waiting on guests out front.

"Hi, Mr. Rick!" La Jetta greeted.

"Hey, Jetta, everything okay?" He asked his new assistant manager. From the beginning, La Jetta had shown herself committed to the business, and he couldn't think of a better person to promote.

"Everything is great," she replied and proceeded to run down the list of messages for him. When she was finished, he went to the back to greet the rest of the crew before heading for his office.

On his way, he passed the small office that Kaycee occupied and he glanced inside. It was strange seeing it dark and cold.

Since their trip, Kaycee had called and told him that she had received some interest in her event-planning skills and she had a couple of new proposals on the table, so she wouldn't be in until the Salsa lesson scheduled for Saturday.

He was happy for her and somewhat relieved to have her out of the way so that he could keep his mind on his work. With her gone, he had been able to focus on detailed reports and documents that required his full attention.

With a sigh he picked up the latest stack of forms and began to pore through them, pushing thoughts of Kaycee out of his mind.

After four intense hours of work in his office, Kendrick stepped out to check on the staff. It was almost three o'clock.

The crowd had tapered down and the staff was preparing for the evening shift.

The first stop was the coffeemaker where he poured himself a cup of black coffee.

The jingling bells at the front door caught his attention and he turned around to find his daughter, Bianca, and grandson, Sebastian.

"Hi, Daddy," she called out as she guided her son through the door.

Kendrick hurried around the counter and scooped Sebastian up in his arms, tickling his ribs. The toddler kicked and giggled with glee at the rough play he enjoyed sharing with his grandfather.

"Hey, baby girl," he returned the greeting. He settled Sebastian in his arms before planting a kiss on her cheek. "What brings you by here?"

"Tim has to work over tonight and I have some depositions I need to clear off my desk and—"

"You need a babysitter," he cut in.

Bianca lowered her head and nodded.

"Didn't I tell you raising kids without family around would be hard?" he gently scolded. "What would you and Tim do without me?"

"That's why I appreciate you so much!" she said hugging him. "I'm so glad you decided to move to Atlanta."

Kendrick placed Sebastian on the floor and he ran around to the back to find his favorite person—La Jetta.

"So, how long do you need me to keep him?"

"Is eight too late?" she asked in her daddy's-little-girl voice coupled with a sweet smile.

Kendrick smiled and shook his head. "Eight is fine."

"Thanks, Dad!"

As he watched her leave, he couldn't help but be reminded of Amanda again. Although her memory held a special place in his heart, she was slipping away. For the first time since her death, another woman was vying for his attention and gaining ground.

Chapter 15

To Kaycee's pleasure, a small crowd had gathered for the free Salsa lessons on Saturday morning. There were four middle-aged couples who appeared to be friends, a group of young women who all belonged to a book club and two guys who happened to be dining in the café and had signed up at the last minute because of the girls. Charlotte served them coffee as they waited for the instructor to arrive.

Stationed at the front counter, Kaycee pored over the monthly calendar. Already she had booked something for every Friday and Saturday. She felt confident that her suggestion to offer more than a cup of coffee and a light meal at Jireh was turning out to be a good one.

The bells on the front door jingled and Kaycee glanced up to find the Peetes, an elderly couple who frequented the café. According to La Jetta, they had been the first customers and because of that, they were entitled to a free cup of coffee every day.

"Good morning, Mr. and Mrs. Peete," she greeted with a smile. "Will you be having the usual today?"

Mr. Peete, a dapper gentleman with a full head of gleaming white hair and a thick matching mustache, chuckled with a twinkle in his eye. "Not today, dear."

"So, you're being adventurous today, huh?" Kaycee teased.

"Actually, sweetie, we're here for the Salsa lessons," Mrs. Peete said with a mischievous glance at her husband. "We figure that maybe we could learn a thing or two to add to our repertoire."

Kaycee's eyes widened with surprise, "Well, alrighty then, why don't you join the others in the back of the dining room? The instructor should be here any minute."

The door opened a second time and in walked a handsome Latino man dressed in a white dress shirt and black trousers. He had a smooth olive complexion with wide clear brown eyes, a hint of five o'clock shadow and a long wavy ponytail that hung to the middle of his back.

"Can I help you?" Kaycee offered.

"Yes, good morning, I'm Hector Reyes. I'm the instructor for the class this morning." He said in perfect English.

Two female customers who were on their way out did a U-turn at hearing that and joined the others in the dining room.

"Hi, Mr. Reyes," Kaycee welcomed him and held out her hand. "I'm Kaycee Jordan. I'm the one who set up the class with your assistant."

Hector's eyes lowered as he took inventory of Kaycee with admiration before resting them back on her face.

"Ms. Jordan, what a pleasure it is to meet you," he replied and raised her hand to his mouth to plant a kiss on the back.

Kaycee was surprised by his action. Maybe hand-kissing was the latest trend.

Apparently, Kendrick thought so, as well. During the exchange, Kaycee hadn't seen him enter the building. The look on his face was a mixture of shock and anger. She could tell by the clenching of his jaw and the muscles flexing beneath his ears.

Neither of them said a word.

Kaycee eased her hand from Hector's grasp. "Mr. Reyes, the class is waiting for you."

Hector could obviously feel the tension between Kaycee and the man with the piercing frown standing stiffly beside them.

"Will you join us?" he asked, stepping into her personal space as if trying to establish territory.

Kaycee smiled and flushed with embarrassment under Kendrick's penetrating gaze.

"No, I have a lot of work to do."

"Please, I think you would be an excellent partner." Quick as a wink, he took her hands and proceeded to do a little move with a gyration of his hips.

Kaycee's brows raised and she looked over at Kendrick who was fuming to the point of blowing his top.

"Mr. Reyes, really," she firmly stated, moving outside of his embrace. "I can't. I have a lot of work, and besides, the group has been waiting for some time. They're eager to get started." She nudged her head toward the people waiting in the dining room. All eyes seemed to be on the three of them, making her flush with embarrassment.

"Okay, *chica*. We will meet again." Hector strolled off with more confidence than Kaycee could bear, leaving her standing face-to-face with Kendrick.

With a frustrated sigh, she turned to look at him. "Good morning, Kendrick."

His face softened at the sweet sound of his name on her tongue.

"You must have the best taste in all of Atlanta," he grunted. "Every time I walk through this door, it seems like someone is kissing you."

"Hello to you, too," she retorted.

He just stood there, shaking his head in disbelief.

"How have you been?" she asked, wanting to step into his arms and bring to reality the embrace that she had been dreaming about since their night in the cabin.

"Apparently, not as good as you."

"Come on, Kendrick," she groaned, growing tired of his jealousy. She wanted to hear him tell her how much he missed her or show her by giving her a kiss, but she knew it wouldn't happen. He remained stock-still with his hands in the pockets of his slacks.

"So this is how you want it to be?" she asked.

Charlotte looked up at the sound of Kaycee's voice rising. Kendrick noticed his employee's attention was on the two of them and cleared his throat.

"May I see you in my office, Ms. Jordan?" he asked, motioning with his head that they had a spectator.

She flashed an irritated frown at him, but in a sweet voice for Charlotte's benefit replied. "Yes, you may."

Kendrick held out his hand, allowing her to go first. Kaycee decided that she was going to make him pay for it. Her asymmetrical black-and-beige, knee-length skirt complemented those womanly assets that she knew Kendrick appreciated so much. Today he would only be allowed to look and not touch!

He said hello to the kitchen staff before going into his office. Kaycee waited for him in the doorway.

"Kendrick, why does this seem like déjà vu?" she asked.

"Why are strange men touching you all of the time?" he shot back, taking a seat.

"It was nothing but a kiss on the hand. He was just flirting."

"That's it? He was just flirting?" He threw his hands in the air. "What if Martinique was back here giving me a neck massage, would that be okay?"

The sound of the woman's name made her flesh curl.

"Please, Kendrick, that's different and you know it. I never had a relationship with either Grant or Hector. You had an outright affair with that woman!"

"It's the same, Kaycee."

"No, it's not," she replied.

"To me, it is."

Kaycee stood silently. While she wished there was something she could do to take back both incidents, she could not.

"Kendrick, I care about you, a lot," she began. "But—"

"Have you planned the dance for this evening?" he cut her off. He didn't know if he could bear hearing anything contrary to the two of them being together.

"I have."

"Will you be here?"

She slowly nodded while wondering why he was behaving in such a manner. "I'm going to run home for a couple of hours, but I'll be back before people arrive."

"Good, I'll see you then," he answered and turned his chair to face the computer screen, virtually shutting down further communication.

When she left the office, Kendrick exhaled, pressing his face into his hands.

After taking care of a few things, Kaycee decided to catch a quick nap before the evening festivities. About an hour into her slumber, the telephone rang. With a stretch she reached over and picked up the telephone. "Kaycee, this is Kendrick."

Kaycee thought she was dreaming. Was he really calling her after another one of their strange altercations?

"Kaycee?"

"Yes?"

"I need you," he said in a thick voice.

Her heart raced. Was she hearing correctly?

"Excuse me?" she asked, wanting to make sure that they were on the same page.

"I need you to come to Jireh," he continued. "There's been an incident."

She sat up in bed. "An incident?"

"Otis fell and sprained his ankle and I got a call that we could expect a group of thirty to come in tonight," he rattled off. "This is in addition to the folks who signed up already. I know you said you were coming, but I really need all hands on deck tonight."

Her first thought was to tell him to call Martinique. After all, she was the "go-to girl", that is, until she saw Kendrick talking to other women. But the urgency in his voice prevented her from making a comment.

"I'll be right there," she heard herself say before she could really think about it.

"Thanks, baby," he murmured. "I'll see you in a little bit."

Baby? Kaycee wasn't sure if she'd heard him correctly, but when she opened her mouth to ask, the line was dead.

As she placed the phone on the hook, she glanced over at the clock. It was almost three o'clock. She didn't plan on going back until six when the crowds would begin pouring in for the authentic Latin cuisine they were preparing.

With a soft sigh, she jumped from the bed and began to get ready.

The staff were buzzing around the kitchen and dining room in preparation for the evening's festivities when Kaycee arrived. After giving her customary greeting to Jaylen, La Jetta and Charlotte, who were managing the front end, she headed straight for the back in search of Kendrick.

The back kitchen staff, with the exception of Otis, were all on point. Food was laid out everywhere. Right in the middle of the room, barking out orders with his elbows deep in ground beef was Kendrick.

Kaycee noticed the stress lining his face the second she entered the room. However, when he turned and his eyes landed on her it melted away.

"Kaycee." He sighed.

"What can I do?" she asked, reaching for a white button-front jacket. She quickly slipped it over her black shirt and black pants, an outfit similar to those worn by the rest of the kitchen staff.

"I'm mixing meat for the empanadas, so if you can whip up the pastry shells, that would be great."

She saluted him and turned on her heels to gather the things she needed.

Everyone worked with concentration and limited conversation. After Kaycee finished the crust for the empanadas, she went right to work on a torte. She later learned that the special guests were from the Black Business Network. She said a silent prayer that Grant would not be one of them because she didn't know if she could take Kendrick, Grant and Hector in the same night.

A few times while she worked with relentless

focus on preparing her dish, she would catch Kendrick watching her. Had she not been so busy, she'd probably wonder what was going on, but she had no time to entertain those thoughts. Not when they had a deadline to meet.

As she cracked the last egg from the clutch in the stainless-steel bowl, she carefully wiped her hands on a towel and headed for the walk-in refrigerator to retrieve some more.

She shivered as the cool air enveloped her, drawing goose bumps. She vigorously rubbed her arms and headed for the area where the eggs were located when she heard the swish of the refrigerator door. She turned around to find Kendrick standing there. They stood there for a few awkward seconds before Kaycee spoke up.

"I'm getting eggs," she announced.

He stepped in closer. "I never thanked you—"

"It's okay," she said with a wave of her hand.

He edged even closer. "I know that I've been acting like a jackass. The last week has been draining. And I, well, I'm sorry, okay?"

Kaycee closed her eyes and nodded slightly, calling a truce. She was getting tired of the emotional roller-coaster ride, as well. She longed for them to spend time just hanging out again.

She opened her eyes to find Kendrick grinning.

"What?" she asked.

"Is it me or is it a little chilly in here for you?" he asked.

"What?"

His eyes lowered seductively to the front of her blouse. Kaycee's eyes dropped in sync to find her nipples poking against the thin material.

With a naughty glint in her eye, she strolled closer to him so that they were mere inches from each other, chest to chest.

"Actually, Kendrick, I'm hot," she purred, her eyes lowered seductively. "Very hot." With that she turned and exited the refrigerator, leaving him wondering what to do next.

Chapter 16

Another successful event at Jireh had brought great reviews in the Living section of the newspaper that Kendrick was reading on his front porch.

The place had been packed, and, as reported, everyone had had a great time. The bookings for special events seemed to increase each day, and Kendrick had Kaycee to thank for it.

It had been her idea to host the Salsa lessons followed by a dance, and he was glad that he had relented and allowed her to broaden his vision to take the café to another level.

The thought of her drew his mind immediately to

their exchange in the refrigerator. Kaycee didn't know it but she was going to have to make a decision soon.

As if he had summoned her, Kaycee appeared on her front walk dressed in a pair of running pants with a matching shirt and sneakers.

Kendrick leaned forward in his seat as he watched her walk to the edge of her driveway swinging her arms.

She stopped and bent over to touch her toes. Holding the stretch for a few seconds, she extended her arms into the air while she leaned her torso to one side and then to the other. She jogged in place for a few seconds and stooped down to tie her shoelace.

Kendrick stood up on his porch, wondering what to say. He really wanted, needed to talk to her. She had been on his mind since last night, and he had to release himself from the feelings swelling inside, but he didn't know how to do it.

It seemed as if every chance he got to break down his feelings to her was foiled by some unexpected scenario.

Kaycee stood and began jogging in place as she waited for a car to pass by. Kendrick's heart raced in his chest. His mouth was as dry as a cotton gin. Stepping off the porch, he started down the walk. It was now or never.

* * *

Kaycee was about to take off down the road when she heard someone call her name. She turned around and smiled when she saw that it was Kendrick. Her eyes glowed with appreciation of his thick build in the black Pittsburgh Steelers jersey and black sweats.

"Hello, neighbor," she greeted.

"Hi, yourself." He held up the paper. "Did you get a chance to read this?"

"Read what?" she asked.

Kendrick proceeded to read the positive review to her.

Kaycee jumped for joy. "Kendrick, I'm so happy for you."

"Without you, it wouldn't have happened," he replied. "Thank you for your suggestions."

"It wasn't me. Jireh was doing well before I even came into the picture."

He shook his head in disagreement. "You made a better impression than I ever could."

The dubious look on Kaycee's face led Kendrick to want to explain further.

"Can we take a walk?" he asked. He held out his hand for her to grasp.

Kaycee hesitated because she was unsure what the gesture meant.

"C'mon, I won't bite," he egged her on and held

it out more directly so that she couldn't mistake his offering for anything else but the fact that he wanted her near to him.

With a slight smile, she reached out and placed her hand in his. He smiled down at her and he began to lead them down the street.

A giddy feeling came over Kaycee. She didn't know what to make of Kendrick's sudden attentiveness, but she enjoyed it very much. It felt so natural, as though their hands were meant to be fitted in such a way.

They walked along silently, pondering their discovery of one another with anticipation and hope.

"So, what do you have planned for today?" he finally asked, breaking both of their private reveries.

"I don't have to go into the restaurant today, do I?" she asked with a sidelong glance.

Kendrick chuckled slightly, realizing where she was headed with her comment. "No, you do not."

"Then I guess I'll do nothing."

The blossoming crape myrtle trees lining the median down the center of the road created a picture of beauty and uniformity. The crape myrtle was one of Kaycee's favorite trees. She already had planting a few on her list of things to have her yardman do before fall set in.

Kendrick noticed her admiration of the landscaping and announced, "They're beautiful."

"What are?"

He pointed to the trees with his free hand. "I love crape myrtles. I'm having some planted this week."

Kaycee immediately stopped in her tracks, preventing them from going farther.

"What's wrong?" Kendrick asked.

"Kendrick, what is this thing with you and me?" she blurted out in frustration.

"What are you talking about?"

"Your comment…the crape myrtles. My yardman is coming…you're planting, too," she blabbered. "It's all making me crazy!"

Kendrick wrapped his arms around her shoulders, pulling her close to him.

Kaycee closed her eyes and melted against his chest. His touch, his scent, all brought up the flood of feelings that she'd had since they'd first met.

"There, there, baby," he whispered. "What's wrong?"

His sweet sentiment caused her to draw back in fear.

"It's that, Kendrick," she replied, stepping out of his hold. "I want to know where we are going. I'm tired of playing these games."

"What games, Kaycee?"

"For starters, you calling me baby and wanting to hold my hand. Then when we get back to Jireh, I'll be back to Ms. Jordan if I say or do something that you don't agree with. I'm not a light switch, Kendrick. I do have feelings."

Kendrick shook his head and slipped his hands into his pants pockets. "I'm sorry that you feel that I'm trying to play games. I'm not."

"Then what do you call it?" she asked, stepping forward with a stern look. "I think I made myself clear on how I felt about you back at the cabin. If you don't want me, then you need to let me know. I've been through this kind of thing already and I don't need to go through it again!"

"What do you want from me, Kaycee?" Kendrick asked.

"What do I want from you?" she shrieked. "What do you want from me? It's more than just me in this."

"You are completely right. I've been doing some serious thinking lately—about us, in fact."

Kaycee's brow raised with apprehension, but she remained silent.

"I've been trying to make sense out of why you and I fight so much, yet we have so much in common." He paused to search her face for confirmation and he could tell she was agreeing with him.

"And I'm tired of fighting. I think we—" before he could finish, a white Volkswagen Passat whipped around the curving street and came to a screeching halt beside them.

Both turned around to find Sidra sitting behind the wheel with a look of urgency on her face.

"Sid?" Kaycee said recognizing the car immediately.

"Kaycee, please get in the car!" Sidra cried.

Kaycee walked to the door. Her eyes widened when she noticed her friend's red and tear-soaked eyes. "What's wrong, Sid?"

Sidra shook her head. "Please get in the car," she repeated. "I *really* need to talk to you."

Kaycee turned back to Kendrick with an apologetic look.

Kendrick returned her stare as if he was willing her to remain with him. Looking back at Sidra, Kaycee couldn't deny the obvious desperation in her friend's eyes. She was in between a rock and a hard place and she didn't know which way to go. Taking both instances into quick consideration, she made a quick decision.

"Kendrick, can we please finish this later?" she asked, not wanting to leave him hanging.

He sighed with frustration and shook his head. "Do whatever you feel is necessary."

She stood for a second looking between the two of them. The two people who she cared about most were trippin'. Both of them were in emotional states and needed her.

"Kaycee can we go—please!" Sidra cried from the driver's seat.

She sighed. "I'll talk with you later, Kendrick, I promise."

Kendrick didn't wait around to reply, he turned on his heel and started jogging away. Kaycee called his name and when he didn't turn around, she got inside the car with a heavy sigh.

She watched from the passenger window as his speed picked up and her heart longed to follow behind him. The resolution was so close and now here she was, back to square one. She continued staring until he turned the corner. When she turned around the first thought that entered her mind was that Sidra had better have a real emergency.

Chapter 17

"Pregnant!"

Sidra responded with a tearful nod of her head.

"Sidra, you are almost thirty years old. How did you slip up and get pregnant, and who's the father?"

Sidra took a deep breath as she held on to the mug of hot coffee with both hands. A wadded tissue was pressed between the mug and her palm to catch the tears that continued to fall.

"It was a mistake. It just happened."

"You weren't using anything?" Kaycee asked.

Sidra shook her head. "I was trying to do the celibacy thing like you."

Kaycee rolled her eyes. Sidra probably didn't know how to spell *vow,* let alone keep one.

"Who's the father?"

Sidra paused for a few seconds before mumbling, "Hampton Barnes."

"Hampton Barnes who was at the Jireh event?"

She hoped she wasn't hearing her friend correctly. Hampton Barnes was an arrogant man who thought he was the master of suaveness. He was also a friend of Paul's and that fact did not score any points with her.

Sidra nodded.

"Have you told him yet?"

She shook her head.

"Are you going to?" She asked the question because she really wanted to know what Sidra intended to do with the baby. Her theory was if you did the crime you needed to do the time.

Sidra shrugged. "I don't know yet. All I know is that I feel so stupid!"

"Why didn't you use protection, Sid?" Kaycee asked. "We always talk about protecting ourselves from diseases. Why didn't you use something?"

Sidra shrugged and wiped her nose. "Things got out of control. Before I knew it, I was naked and we were rolling all over the bed. Protection slipped my mind."

"And now you're going to be a mother," Kaycee said. She wasn't getting bent out of shape by the fact that her friend was with child. What bothered her was the fact that Sidra was a professional woman with common sense. She was also a woman who desired a family, yet had no prospects for a husband. In the back of her mind, she couldn't help but wonder if her friend had put herself in this position on purpose.

"Look, whatever you decide to do, I'll support you," Kaycee announced. "But you do know my feelings toward abortion. I want no part of that."

"I'm not going to have an abortion," Sidra emphatically replied.

"Then what will you do?" Kaycee asked.

Sidra shrugged her shoulders. "I guess I'll have to have it."

Kaycee snorted, "Yeah, right, you hardly take good care of yourself."

Sidra's head dropped to the side as though she couldn't believe that Kaycee had said that.

"Excuse me, but I am a grown woman. I can make decisions for myself."

"You're right," Kaycee said and leaned over to give her friend a hug. "I'm sorry, girl, it's just that I can't believe this."

"You? How do you think I feel?" Sidra buried her face in her hands. "So much for living the single life."

Kaycee stroked her back. "We will get through this, Sid. I will support you in every way that I can, I promise. Children are not accidents, they are gifts from God."

Sidra curled up on the sofa, embraced one of the throw pillows and yawned.

"Kaycee, I know I say and do some really stupid things, but thanks for being my friend anyway."

"Don't mention it," Kaycee replied.

"Will you pray for me?" Sidra whispered sleepily.

Kaycee was surprised by her friend's request. Sidra had always opposed anything dealing with the church, which surprised Kaycee because her friend was a preacher's kid. But Kaycee was no angel herself even though growing up in Katherine and Russell's home had meant everybody went to church.

Kaycee had been obedient, but when she went off to college, the party life consumed her and she turned away from her parents' ways. It wasn't until she and Paul got together that she began to go again. However, the church Paul attended wasn't necessarily her cup of tea. Everything seemed to be based more on what you had than on who you were and that disturbed Kaycee. She didn't want to be known by the pastor only because she was one of the largest tithers in the house.

Since her breakup with Paul, she had visited a few churches here and there, but she hadn't found the one she was looking for. Kaycee walked over and kneeled on the floor beside the sofa where Sidra lay.

She wasn't perfect, either. She made many mistakes, but Sidra needed her. She closed her eyes and said a silent prayer for her friend.

Chapter 18

There would be no conversation with Kendrick that evening. When Kaycee finally got Sidra calmed down, the two hung out for a while. By the time Sidra went home, it was late. Kaycee called Kendrick the second Sidra backed out the driveway, but his phone just rang. She tried to call him twice before she went to bed but she still couldn't reach him.

Sleep evaded Kaycee. Her thoughts were on the man who played lead role in her dreams.

Jireh's morning crowd had grown into a comfortable mixed crowd of regulars: early-morning walkers, senior citizens, self-employed business owners and college students.

Kaycee recognized many of them as she entered the front door and greeted them with a hello and a warm smile. After exchanging pleasantries with La Jetta and Nichole, who were working the front end, she took a deep breath and headed toward the back.

Melody was busy prepping vegetables for salads while Rafael busied himself with side dishes. Otis sat on a stool propped up before a table where he was going over paperwork and barking out orders.

"Hi, Ms. Kaycee," Melody greeted.

"Hi, Melody, how are you?"

"Could be better."

A concerned frown lined Kaycee's forehead. "What's going on?"

Melody shook her head. "It's not me you should be worried about."

"What are you talking about?" Kaycee asked.

Melody stepped closer. "Everybody trippin' around here and I'm just keeping to myself because the air is negative."

"Negative?" Kaycee repeated.

Melody nudged her head toward the back. "First it was Mr. Otis. He came up in here acting like a grouch, but I know he got good reason because he hurt his ankle and all, but Mr. Rick is another story. He came up in here, didn't say good morning or nothing.

When I went back there to talk to him, he advised me to go back to the kitchen."

"He said that?" Kaycee asked in disbelief. Despite how much the staff tried Kendrick he never lost his cool.

Melody nodded. "So, I'm going to stay in here and do my work, then go home."

Kaycee looked toward the offices and shook her head. She had a good idea why he was acting that way.

"Don't worry, Melody, we'll work it out."

Just at that moment the office door opened and Kendrick stormed out. His eyes surveyed the room before stopping on Kaycee. The gentleness that she was accustomed to seeing was missing, replaced by a coldness as he looked her up and down.

"Where's your uniform?"

"What uniform?" Kaycee asked. She had never been required to wear one before.

"Everyone in the back kitchen must wear a white smock."

"Since when?"

"Since always," he replied. "Get a smock, Ms. Jordan."

He walked away before Kaycee could get a word in. Melody gave her an I-told-you-so look.

With an exasperated sigh, Kaycee trudged off in search of a smock. On the way, anger and frustration built up inside. She knew that Kendrick's distant behavior had a lot to do with her choosing to stay with

Sidra over him the previous day. It wasn't as though she hadn't tried to make contact with him afterwards.

The rest of that day, the back of the restaurant resembled a communist sweat shop. The tone had been set. There was no talking, only production. Kendrick saw to it by emerging from his office every so often to comment if it looked like they were off task. By lunchtime, he had to don a smock himself and jump in due to Otis's inability to move around.

Kendrick and Kaycee worked side by side without exchanging a word. The tension was so thick it could be cut with a knife.

A couple of times they bumped hands reaching for the same utensil, but rather than apologize as they normally would have, they continued to work in silence. When Kendrick had to reach for a pan above the area where Kaycee was working, he accidentally bumped into her again. Kaycee looked up at him as if waiting for him to apologize, but he only returned her stare. Finally, she rolled her eyes and moved out of the way.

After the lunch crowd had tapered down, Melody went on lunch and Otis went home. Rafael stepped out in the back to smoke a cigarette, leaving Kendrick and Kaycee in the kitchen.

Kaycee was in the middle of frosting a cake. She was so engrossed in what she was doing she did not notice Kendrick approaching her from behind.

It wasn't until she felt him standing close behind her that she inhaled a quick breath. Rather than acknowledge his presence, she continued working without a word.

Kendrick slid his arms around her waist, fitting her body tightly against his and placed a kiss on the back of her neck. His tender act caused her to exhale. She didn't like being mad at him.

His hands moved up to her waist where he gently turned her around so that they were facing each other. There was no need for words, for their eyes showed it all. The pain, the exhaustion, the love, the apology.

He slowly lifted her onto the work table and wrapped her in his arms. Kaycee closed her eyes, savoring his touch. She needed his touch. They pulled apart, but their lips moved closer together like magnets until they met with an electrifying kiss.

What had started out as a gentle brush of lips against lips quickly turned deep, passionate and needy.

A guttural groan escaped Kaycee's throat as he teased her, pleased her and eased her with tongue skills that promised more, had they been in another place.

Bracing himself firmly between her thighs, Kendrick pulled her tightly against him and kissed her forehead.

"I hate it when we fight."

"Me, too," she murmured, caressing his back. "I'm sorry for leaving you."

"You were just being a good friend. I can't be mad for that. Is she okay?"

Kaycee looked up at him with love-filled eyes. "I don't want to talk about Sidra right now. It's all about you and me."

Kendrick chuckled. "We better stop before somebody walks in on us."

"Frankly, my dear, I don't give a damn," Kaycee replied, borrowing the line from *Gone With the Wind.*

"I know, I would like to spend some time with you. How about I come over tonight?"

Kaycee's face lit up, "I would love that!"

"I'll drop by around eight," he said, and covered her mouth with his own once again to taste the sweet nectar beyond her lush lips.

At that moment the back door opened. Kaycee jumped off of the table and scrambled away from Kendrick. She turned her back to make it seem like she was working on something.

Rafael entered. He looked at Kendrick then at Kaycee and back to Kendrick and smiled knowingly.

"Ms. Kaycee," he called out her name.

Kaycee spun around. "Yes, Rafael?"

"It appears you have some frosting on the back of your smock," he announced, walking past her toward the dining room.

Kaycee flushed with embarrassment. When

Rafael disappeared behind the door, the two fell against each other in silent laughter.

"We would make terrible secret agents," Kaycee whispered. "The British Secret Service would not have either of us."

Kendrick nodded in agreement as he held her against him, not wanting to depart from her touch.

He pressed his lips against hers again, "I... can't...stop."

"I know," she murmured against his neck, her tongue tasting the sweet warmth. "But we have to."

He pulled back, his breath ragged. "I think it's probably best that you go home. Get some rest and I'll be there tonight, okay?"

"Okay," she replied. They exchanged one more kiss before pulling apart. Kaycee's legs felt like jelly as she walked away, all the while knowing that this night would be the one to change things between them forever.

Chapter 19

At eight on the nose, Kaycee's doorbell rang. Before answering, she padded across the plush carpet in her bare feet to the guest bath for a final check in the mirror.

The simple beige silk spaghetti-strap dress with flowing skirt looked both romantic and comfortable and complemented the wet-look curly hairstyle she'd chosen. She topped off her look with a pink-and-beige orchid pinned in her hair.

Soft music and candlelight provided the perfect backdrop for a romantic evening. Kendrick had called ahead to let her know that he was bringing the food and she'd told him that she would provide the dessert. What he didn't know was that dessert lay beneath the folds of her dress.

She opened the door and smiled at the sight of him standing there as he had before, laden with bags but this time also carrying a dozen red roses.

"For me!" she squealed with excitement. Instinctively they leaned in at the same time for a kiss as if they'd been doing it forever.

"You look really good," he commented, stepping back to admire her.

Kaycee blushed. "Thanks. You look pretty good yourself."

His orange shirt complemented his bronze complexion but its pairing with the casual black slacks did justice to his powerful build.

She took his hand and led him into the family room where a romantic setting for two awaited them. The coffee table was laid out Japanese-style with red silk oriental placemats and matching throw pillows on the floor for seating. The only lighting was generated by two slender candles in the center of the table and the fire in the gas fireplace.

Kendrick placed the bag on the table.

"You know, it seems like you're always bringing me food," Kaycee teased, sidling up beside him like a playful girl. "What do you have in there?"

"I picked up a little something from one of my

favorite restaurants," he replied as he reached inside the bag. "We have salmon pizza, creamy curry soup, grilled fresh fruit—and to drink—white cranberry mojitos!"

She smacked her lips. "Sounds delicious."

Kendrick was about to lay out the spread when he noticed that neo-soul artist Kem's CD was playing.

He paused, his eyes lighting up, "Don't tell me you like Kem, too?"

"I love Kem. Have you seen him in concert?"

Kendrick nodded, "I caught him at the jazz series at Stone Mountain."

"Me, too!" Kaycee said, amazed once more by another shared interest.

Before she could think about it, Kendrick took her hand and pulled her into his arms for a slow dance in the middle of the floor.

His actions caught her off guard. Being spontaneously pulled into dance was not something that happened to her every day. When the song ended and another began, his pace slowed down.

"You know, this song has a lot of meaning to me," he announced in a whisper.

"How so?"

"Because it reminds me of something familiar."

"And what would that be?"

"Us," he replied.

Kaycee paused, wondering if her ears had deceived her.

"Us?"

Kendrick proceeded to explain by reciting the lyrics as Kem sang. Each time he sang a line, Kaycee would cut in with a comment.

"But when we met, neither of us was acting perfect," she replied in response to the line about meeting the perfect stranger. She recollected stumbling around on one stiletto. Never would she have guessed that a situation so negative would have drawn them so close together.

Kendrick continued singing about how the sun was shining on Kaycee.

"But it was dark out," she interjected.

He ignored her comment and stated how the Lord was smiling on him.

Kaycee sighed with a sweet smile. "He was?"

He finished with the chorus which also happened to be the title of the song, stressing the words that he couldn't stop loving her. His words tapered off as he stared deeply into her eyes, letting Kaycee know that he was very serious.

Her breath caught as his confession pierced her heart and illuminated her body like a ray of sunshine. Feelings of joy and contentment lifted her. She paused before returning the sentiment wanting to make sure that she wasn't just imagining anything and that they were both on the same page.

"Did you say what I think you said?" she asked.

He nodded.

"You…you're saying you love me?" she asked softly, wanting confirmation.

He closed his eyes and slowly nodded. "I don't know when it happened, but you were right when you said that everything about us seems so right. I think that's when I knew I loved you, too."

With that he lowered his head and pressed his mouth sweetly against hers. Kaycee exhaled as he moved his mouth to trail kisses down her jawline and neck.

"I wanted to tell you that day when your friend came over and interrupted our talk," he murmured against her skin between kisses. "I've tried everything to convince myself that it couldn't work. The age difference, our working relationship—but I couldn't stop my feelings. Truth is, Kaycee Jordan, I can't get over you no matter what I do. So I'm not going to fight it any longer. We have something special and we deserve to allow it to grow. I want to give it a chance."

Kissing him softly, she cradled his head against her own. Their bodies swayed only slightly to the beat as they absorbed the lyrics to the song as if Kem was performing it just for them!

When the song ended, Kaycee took Kendrick's hand, brought it to her mouth and kissed the back before placing it on her breast where her heart beat rapidly underneath.

"You got it now."

His brow raised in uncertainty, he asked, "What do you mean?"

"You got my heart," she whispered. "And with it comes my complete love and devotion."

"Then I guess I better take care of it," he said, leaning over to kiss the warm skin on her shoulders where his hand had rested moments earlier. He continued planting slow, deliberate kisses on her neck and bare shoulder where he proceeded to tease the spaghetti strap down with his teeth.

He smoothed his hands over her silky shoulders so that both straps now dangled, threatening to release the flimsy material and display her nakedness.

With seductive eyes, Kaycee took Kendrick by the hand. "Show me how you can take care of me," she challenged.

She led him over to the fireplace. Along the way, she retrieved the pillows from the table, and laid them before the hearth. Holding his hand, she lowered herself to the floor on top of the pillows.

Kendrick reached to unbutton his shirt, but Kaycee leaned up on her knees and grabbed his hands before he could begin. She then pulled him down to his knees so that they were kneeling before each other.

Slowly she began unbuttoning his shirt. When the last button came undone, she pressed her hands against the silky hairs on his rippling abdomen and slid them up to his sculpted chest.

She knew that Kendrick had a nice build because his clothes seemed to fit him well, but the proof was seeing it without covering. She shivered with delight, deciding right away that she loved his body. At forty-eight, Kendrick had a body that could give any man half his age a run for the money.

She leaned forward and kissed him in the center of his chest, her tongue swirling through the soft hairs. Kendrick groaned and reached to pull her into his arms, but Kaycee caught his hands in her own. She held them to his side while she continued tasting him.

Glancing down between them, she could see that he was ready to receive her. With a naughty glint in her eye, she lowered the straps of her dress to reveal her full breasts, swollen with desire. His breath caught as her soft flesh melted against his when she closed the space between them.

When he tried to reach for her again, Kaycee stopped him by entwining her fingers with his. She rained kisses up his arm onto his shoulder and across his chest before capturing his mouth with a sexy bite.

"Stop teasing me, woman," he groaned.

"Am I teasing you?" she asked with a swirl of her tongue.

Kendrick couldn't take it any longer and responded by freeing his hands and pulling her into his embrace. He repositioned their bodies so that they were lying on the floor with him leaning over her. He looked down into Kaycee's beautiful face as feelings of love flooded his mind and heart.

"Kaycee, I love you." He kissed her, the realization both exciting and frightening him. He'd never thought he could start over following his wife's death, but with Kaycee he could see a whole new chapter of his life unfolding and he wanted to pursue it with all that he had. "I really love you."

"I love you, too," she whispered.

With skillful hands, Kendrick slid the dress over her hips and was surprised to find her wearing nothing more than a string as a pair of panties.

"What the—"

"You like your dessert?" she asked with a playful smile.

"Yes!" he emphatically replied.

He quickly tossed his shirt to the side and undid his pants, kicking them across the room. When they were both finally free, they began to explore each other with kisses and caresses, savoring the feel and touch of each other's bodies.

Kendrick was gentle, especially when he dared to explore her most secret place. It was a journey Paul had refused to take, but one that Kendrick traveled with boldness and much skill. He made Kaycee feel like a prize the way he handled her. He was slow and tender, making sure that she received every bit of enjoyment in the process.

Kaycee had never known what she was missing. She felt as if she was being sucked up into a cyclone, spiraling out of control then knocked totally immobile. When Kendrick gripped her hips and proceeded to do some things with his tongue, Kaycee thought she was going to disintegrate. She couldn't describe what was happening because her tongue was tied from the blissful fire burning in the core of her body.

Kendrick moved away for a few minutes to protect them both by slipping on a condom. When he returned, he kissed his way back up her body until he reached her mouth where he kissed her deep and hard.

Instinctively, Kaycee braced herself to receive all of him. Although he had waited for this moment, Kendrick took his time. He wanted them both to savor the feel. He eased himself in, then out several times until she begged him to stay. Finally, when Kaycee couldn't take his teasing any longer, she locked her legs around his, causing them to connect deeper. The impact made her see stars.

With the hardness and vigor of youth, Kendrick made love to her as though their lives depended on it. Kaycee quickly picked up his rhythm and matched his strokes with her own. Suddenly her body trembled, unrestrained yet totally satisfied, leaving her murmuring Kendrick's name over and over and over again. In the intimate glow of the firelight, man and woman became one.

Chapter 20

Kaycee stretched and yawned as she crossed over from sleep to consciousness. Ordinarily, she was bothered by the sunlight shining through her window, but not today. A satisfied smile spread across her face as she remembered her night with Kendrick.

She reached to the other side of the bed for his warm body and was surprised to find it empty. Her eyes popped open when her hand came in contact with the rumpled bedding where he had lain the night before.

Rolling onto her side, Kaycee looked toward the door to find him sitting in the chair across the room.

They exchanged warm smiles before she eased back down under the covers.

"What are you doing way over there?" she asked and beckoned for him to return to her. "Come back over here."

"I was just watching you sleep," he replied, lying down beside her. He pulled her against his chest.

He caressed her back. "I know you didn't think I'd left you."

She shrugged. "I didn't know what to think."

He stopped stroking to peer down at her. "Has that happened to you before?"

"It has," she whispered with a nod.

"Tell me about it," he replied, pulling her tighter in his arms as if to protect her from further pain. "I want to know everything about you."

"Those are the kind of memories I prefer to forget," she snorted.

"We should never regret our past," he said. "Besides, now that we are going to start seeing each other, it's necessary that we clear up our pasts so we can move forward."

She shrugged. "What would you like to know?"

"Has the situation with Paul soured your outlook on marriage and relationships?"

"I accepted our incompatibility long before we split. So I've had plenty of time to heal from the separation." She looked up at him. "What about you? I know your wife passed a few years ago, but have you moved on from that yet?"

He hesitated before answering. What he and Amanda had shared was special, but he had asked for honesty so he had to give it in return.

"I must admit that I'm still affected by her passing, but I know I don't like being alone."

"Kendrick, do I remind you of her?"

He hesitated, realizing that he had to choose the right words. "In some ways you do. You both have a fighting spirit. But you have a way about yourself that is unique. You are confident and you know how to have real fun. I admire your ability to say exactly what's on your mind without hurting a person's feelings. I also like how you don't let social mores hold you back from what you want. That's what I love most about you."

His complete acceptance of who she was touched her heart deeper than he would ever know. Tears clouded her eyes as she squeezed him tightly.

The day was dedicated to their newfound love. Kendrick decided that they both should take a day off from work so that they could spend quality time together.

Kaycee took on the duty of planning their day. After they'd shared a hot shower where they engaged in heated lovemaking once more, Kaycee slipped into a pale-yellow sleeveless dress with a flirty flouncing hemline and a pair of sexy strappy sandals with a rosette on the toes and ties up at the ankles.

"Where are we going that we have to dress up?" Kendrick asked, stepping up to embrace her from behind.

"It's a surprise," she told him and fought not to close her eyes and sink into his possession again. She quickly regained composure and turned around to inspect him.

"We need to go over to your house," she announced, her eyes skimming over the previous evening's now-wrinkled shirt and pants.

"Where are we going again?" he asked as they exited her front door hand in hand to go to his place.

"It's a surprise."

"I should know so I'll know what to wear."

"Just pick out something dressy casual."

Kendrick opened the door and allowed her to enter the quiet house before him.

Kaycee looked around expecting to see Tiki running up to greet them, but when it didn't happen she turned to Kendrick with questioning eyes.

"She finally went back home."

"Your daughter picked her up?"

He nodded. Then pulled her close to him, wrapping her in his arms. "You know, we're going to have christen my place now."

Kaycee laughed. "I haven't seen your place. Why don't you give me a tour?"

"Help yourself," he replied "while I run up and get ready."

"Okay." She knew his taste at Café Jireh and was curious to see if it matched that in his home. She watched him bound up the stairs before taking her self-guided tour.

In his office, which held a large desk, a credenza, a loveseat and chairs and bookshelves, Kaycee spotted some framed photos. Curious about them, she stepped across to the shelves to investigate. There were pictures of a younger Kendrick with a little girl who, except for missing front teeth and shoulder-length ponytails, was his spitting image. Pictures of his daughter showed her in different stages of her life, including high-school graduation, her wedding and a family photo.

Next she came upon a picture of him dressed in his Steelers uniform with two other players, apparently after winning a conference game. There were pictures of Kendrick with local celebrities like Evander Holyfield and Monica Kaufman.

Traveling down the rows of photos, she came across an obviously older picture of Kendrick with a beautiful young woman that she guessed was Amanda. There were others of the two of them and then one of Amanda in her later years, looking just as beautiful as she had in her youth.

With a sigh, Kaycee stepped out of the room and went to the other parts of the home.

The dining room was simple, with a mahogany table with eight high-back, black-leather chairs and a matching buffet.

The kitchen was clean and although it had the same layout as hers, it displayed a difference in taste with darker cabinets and countertops and Mexican-tile floors. Like her, Kendrick appeared to do most of his living in the family room, which was warm and cozy with an inviting lived-in quality.

She turned on her heel and headed upstairs in search of the room that she was most curious about.

The second level differed from Kaycee's home in that there were only three bedrooms compared to her four. She headed straight for the double doors at the end of the hall; that was where her bedroom was also located. She toyed with the idea of just walking in, but decided against it and knocked instead.

"Kendrick."

She pressed her ear against the door and could make out the sound of water running and music playing.

Kaycee knocked a little harder. "Kendrick!"

"Yes!" he shouted back.

"Are you almost ready?" She couldn't wait to tell him that her surprise would be a day spent at Château Elan where they would dine in the Versailles restaurant, visit the winery and take pleasure in his and hers salon treatments at the spa. It was something that she had longed to do with Paul, but he had never had an interest.

"Come in!" he called back.

She turned the knob and stepped inside his bedroom.

"Hello?" she sang as she inched into the spotless, spacious room.

"I'm in the bathroom," he called back.

Kaycee went directly to the bathroom where she found him wearing nothing more than a towel around his waist.

"I've been waiting for you," he announced through smoldering eyes. At that moment, he released the towel from his hips, exposing his naked glory, ready and waiting.

Her eyes traveled down the full length of him, and she smiled appreciatively at his sheathed member swollen with desire. "You have, haven't you?"

He nodded and slowly walked toward her until they were a breath away from each other. He pulled her by the hips against his hardness. "We have to christen my house, remember."

With a swift motion, Kendrick scooped her up in his arms, so that she was straddling him. He backed her up against the closed door for leverage. Smoothing his hand up her thigh, he lifted the skirt of her dress so that it encircled her waist, leaving her panties as the only barrier between them. With skillful hands, he maneuvered the delicate fabric to the side before entering her with a satiated groan.

Kaycee had never realized that making love in a standing position could be so satisfying. In fact, it enhanced her arousal, causing her to do and say things to Kendrick that she wouldn't have ordinarily. The rumbling feeling deep in her belly quickly grew into an outright roar and she screamed as she collapsed against him. Kendrick soon followed with his own release. Afterwards, they slid down the door to the bathroom floor, kissing each other all over.

Château Elan was the furthest thing from either of their minds.

Chapter 21

"Daddy!"

Kendrick thought he was dreaming and rolled over onto his back.

"Daddy, are you here?"

He stirred in his sleep at the sound of his daughter, Bianca's, familiar voice.

He groaned and looked over at the clock on his nightstand. It was almost seven o'clock in the evening.

A soft rap on his door made him sit up. When he did, he felt the familiar warm body that he had been almost literally glued to for the last twenty-four hours. Looking down, his eyes fell upon Kaycee sleeping peacefully on her stomach with her arms wrapped around a pillow.

"Dad."

"I'm coming, B," he called back.

Kaycee stirred, her eyes fluttering open.

"Mmm," she moaned. "Did you say something, baby?"

"No, go back to sleep."

"Dad, are you okay?" Bianca asked.

"Yes, baby. Give me a minute and I'll be down," Kendrick replied.

Kaycee's eyes opened and she quickly covered herself. "Who is that?"

"It's my daughter, Bianca," he replied, swinging his legs over the edge of the bed. The cool air hit his skin and he yearned for the warmth created by their bodies in the sheets.

"Oh, my goodness, Kendrick, what is she going to think?" Kaycee asked with alarm.

"Don't worry," he replied, reaching for a pair of jeans and a T-shirt discarded on a nearby chair. "I'll handle it, but since you're here, you might as well get up and meet her."

Kaycee's eyes popped open. "You've got to be kidding?"

"No, I'm not. Why shouldn't you two meet? You're going to have to one day."

"Can it be another day?" Kaycee asked.

"Daddy, are you alone?" Bianca called out.

Both of their heads turned to look at the other in surprise. Kendrick had thought Bianca had gone downstairs. He should have remembered how stubborn and nosey his daughter could be. He believed these qualities made her a great attorney.

"Bianca, I thought I asked you to go downstairs!" he barked.

"I'm not a child!" she shouted back.

Kendrick sauntered over to the bedroom door and yanked it open just as Kaycee pulled the covers over her head.

"You're right, you are not a child which is why you shouldn't be standing at this door eavesdropping."

"I'm not eavesdropping. I heard talking and I came back to the door because I thought you were talking to me."

"Well, I wasn't," he replied, slipping the T-shirt over his head. "I'll—no, *we'll* be down in a few minutes."

Bianca's eyes traveled beyond his strong shoulder and narrowed in anger when they came back to rest on him. Kendrick knew she had an attitude, but he also knew she had better get over it. Since Amanda had died, his daughter had seemed bent on hindering any relationship he could have. It might have worked with some of the other women, but it wouldn't with Kaycee.

She shook her head with a pathetic look on her

face and rolled her eyes. "I'll be downstairs." She turned on her heel and traipsed down the stairs.

Kendrick waited for her to reach the landing below before closing the door again.

"I'm sorry about that, baby," he apologized. "She acts like she can control this part of my life, but don't worry, I won't let her."

"Kendrick, this is so embarrassing," Kaycee said from under the blankets.

He lifted the covers. "Kaycee, it's out now. You and I are in love and everybody around us is just going to have to accept it."

His strong words of conviction pierced her heart. He was right. They couldn't deny their love. With a kiss on his mouth, she got out of bed. Kendrick went downstairs to talk to Bianca while she showered and dressed. When she felt presentable enough, Kaycee exited the bedroom to join them.

Bianca's back was to her when she entered the family room. Kendrick saw her approaching and stood up to met her. As a show of support, he put his arm around her waist.

When she saw her father jump up from his seat, Bianca must have known it was showtime. Clearing her throat, she stood up and turned around. When she saw Kaycee enter the room her mouth fell open.

"Bianca, I want you to meet Kaycee Jordan. Kaycee, this is my daughter, Bianca Mills."

Kaycee held out her hand. "Hi, Bianca. It's good to meet you finally. I've heard so much about you."

Bianca returned a weak handshake. "I'm sorry I can't say the same. I guess my father's been keeping you under wraps."

Kaycee gave Kendrick a curious glance, but said nothing.

"Bianca," he said in a warning kind of way. Taking Kaycee's hand in his, Kendrick led her over to the sofa.

"So Bianca, how are Tim and Sebastian?" he asked, referring to his son-in-law and grandson as if this meeting was a small thing.

"Daddy, they are fine, but they are not the issue right now. I don't mean to be rude, Kaycee, but, Daddy, don't you think I deserve some kind of explanation?"

"Bianca, last I checked I was the parent," he said sternly.

Kaycee tapped his hand before he could go on. "Kendrick, she's right. Like you said, you and I are in love and we owe it to the people who love us to let them know."

Kendrick grumbled in protest, but conceded in honor of Kaycee's wishes.

"Bianca, like Kaycee said, we are seeing each other."

"Since when?"

"Officially since last night but we've known each other for some time now."

Bianca pursed her lips and rolled her eyes. "Kaycee, exactly how old are you anyway?"

"Age doesn't make a difference," Kendrick quickly cut in.

"Is it a problem for me to know?" Bianca asked.

"No it's not," Kaycee replied. "I'm twenty-nine, Bianca."

She watched as the younger woman's lips twisted in disapproval. "Okay, now do you realize that I am twenty-five?"

Kaycee nodded indifferently. "I'm aware of your age."

Bianca stood from her perch on the edge of the sofa and walked across the room. "You're also aware that my father is almost fifty?"

"I am."

"Bianca Shalon, I will not have you interrogating Kaycee like she's on the witness stand!" Kendrick barked.

"Daddy, what is going on in your head?" Bianca shouted, pointing at Kaycee as if she were an ornament in the room. "She is young enough to be my sister. What are you going to do with a girl?"

"She's not a girl, she's a woman!" he corrected her.

"She is nineteen years younger than you!"

"So what!" Kendrick boomed. "If you would give

her a chance you would see that she is very intelligent, she's kind, unselfish and we are compatible in so many ways."

Kaycee could feel the heat stirring in her abdomen from his complimentary words. It was moments like this that made her know her feelings for him were so right.

"So what are you going to do if she wants to get married and have babies?" Bianca shot back.

Their eyes immediately connected because it was a topic that neither of them had bothered to discuss. Bianca could sense their trepidation and decided to play it in her favor.

"Are you ready to be changing diapers at fifty?" she queried. Then she turned to Kaycee. "What about when his bum knee really goes out and he can't move around as much? Would it cramp your style to have a cripple for a husband?"

"Bianca, I'm going to have to ask you to leave!" Kendrick broke in. He jumped up from his seat, stomped to the door and opened it. "I'm sorry, baby, but you will have to understand that this is the woman I love and I intend to be with her."

Bianca looked from one to the other and sighed in defeat. With a lowered head, she gathered her purse and walked to the door. Before she crossed the threshold she turned back to Kendrick.

"I pray that you will open your eyes and see the mistake you're making."

Kendrick quietly closed the door behind her and turned around to find a stunned Kaycee. He wanted to take away the whole incident with his stubborn daughter. Kaycee was a strong-willed person, but he believed that Bianca had her beat.

"Come here, baby," he said, opening his arms for her.

Kaycee ran into them and pressed her face against his chest.

"That didn't go over so well," she said with a sigh.

"Don't worry about Bianca," he said as he intimately stroked the nape of her neck with his palm. "Her bark is far worse than her bite."

"Kendrick, do you think we're making a mistake?" she asked looking up into his eyes, searching for the answer to calm her fears.

"No, I don't," he answered and kissed her nose. "We belong together."

Kaycee hugged him tightly, trying to get the assurance that she desperately wanted and needed. She loved Kendrick Thompson to the point that she knew it would hurt not to have him in her life.

Chapter 22

Since their first night together, Kendrick and Kaycee had been inseparable. In both of their eyes it was only natural to want to be with each other 24/7. Therefore, their days started wrapped in each other's arms and their nights the same.

It wasn't a sex thing, either. Although their physical attraction to each other was high, their desire included companionship, friendship and shared interests.

If they were not holding each other as they slept, they were sitting on the edge of the bed watching Thursday—and Sunday—night football. Other nights were spent reading to each other. Kaycee, who claimed she never had time to read, looked forward to listening to Kendrick's deep voice as he read from his latest novel of choice. It was like a book on tape but in real time.

Neither could believe that happiness on such a level existed. To find "the one" who was your match totally and completely was the greatest blessing of all.

Following breakfast, they gathered their things to leave for work. They thought it was best to continue to drive in separate cars so that the staff would not get suspicious about their relationship. It wasn't that they were hiding it, but they wanted to tell them at the right time.

Like a gentleman, Kendrick pulled Kaycee's Toyota out of the garage and had it warmed and ready for her when she exited the house through the open garage door.

He opened the driver's door for her and held her hand as she stepped up in her heels to get inside.

"Thanks, baby," she said, giving him a kiss.

"No, thank you," he replied.

She looked at him curiously, "For what?"

"For wearing that skirt," he said, smoothing his hand up the smooth plane of her calf and thigh. "I've been watching you all morning. If I didn't have a ten o'clock meeting, I would march you back in that house and let you have it."

She giggled at the thought of being made to go in

the house and undress. She wouldn't mind it, either. The thought actually made her heart race.

"Don't make promises that you can't keep," she warned. "You're not going to do anything but be on fire all day. It would be embarrassing for you to walk around in front of your colleagues in that condition."

He grunted. "I have more control than that."

"Do you now?" she challenged, sliding her arms around his neck. She met his lips with her own. Her kiss was deep, passionate and as needy as if they had all the time in the world.

It was amazing how something as simple as her kiss made him weak. Kissing Kaycee was more than just a show of emotion. It was a prelude to something more than just sex. It was communication on a whole different level, an understanding and a branding of some sort all rolled in one. Kendrick was claiming her and she was a marked woman.

Finally, after a few minutes, he pulled back. Kaycee sat there looking as if she was spinning but trying to regain control by fanning herself.

Kendrick chuckled as he reached up to finger one of the curls on her head. "Are you okay?"

With her eyes still closed she nodded without a word.

"Are you sure?"

Kaycee's eyes slowly opened. "We need to stop."

"You started something now," he said, playfully trying to reach for her again.

"And you have a very important meeting. We will continue this later," she said with a tug on his shirt.

Kendrick reached inside the vehicle and attached her seat belt.

"Thank you."

He kissed her on the cheek. "I just want to make sure my woman is safe."

They kissed once more and departed in separate vehicles.

As she backed out of the driveway, Kaycee thought about how much her life had changed in the last few months. She thought about how their paths had crossed and she hadn't been able to look away since. She couldn't imagine her life before Kendrick had come into her world. He was so much the perfect fit that it sometimes scared her.

The ringing of the telephone disrupted her thoughts. She reached for it and immediately recognized her parents' home number.

"Hello," she sang into the phone.

"Hey, baby girl." It was her mother.

"Hi, Mom."

"Are you busy?"

"Just on my way to work."

"I was just calling to let you know that your dad and I will be in town next week."

"You will?" she exclaimed. "When are you coming?" She hoped it didn't clash with an affair that Kendrick had invited her to attend. It would be their first time out as a couple and she was looking forward to meeting his colleagues.

"On the twenty-third, but most of our time will be spent at a hotel."

Kaycee gasped in disappointment. "Why?"

"It's sort of like a class reunion. A bunch of us from our old high school are getting together for a dinner cruise on Lake Lanier. We got a weekend package deal at a resort there, too."

"Will I see you guys?"

"Of course," her mother exclaimed. "We're going to extend our trip to hang out with you for a few extra days."

"Good, I would hate for you to come all this way and then not see you."

"I'll call you when we get to Atlanta, okay?"

"Okay," she replied. After exchanging a few more pleasantries, they hung up.

Kaycee was excited about her parents coming, but she was also nervous. She didn't know how they would react to Kendrick. He was only a few years younger than they were.

For the most part, they were fair and even-tempered, which was why she admired and respected them so much. She was sure that after they got past the age difference with Kendrick, they would zero in on the one thing that all parents wished and hoped for for their child and that was that he loved her unconditionally and made her happy. She'd found that in Kendrick Thompson, and she was sure they would see that, also.

After the lunch crowd had tapered off, Kaycee took the time to go out into the dining area to place table tents announcing a book signing for a local author.

Along the way she greeted the customers and even stopped to chat with some. She had just finished the last table and gone back to the counter when Sidra entered the café.

"Sid, hey," she greeted her friend with a hug.

"Hey, girl, you got a minute?"

"Sure," Kaycee assured her. "Would you like something to eat?"

Sidra peered into the dessert case. "That red velvet cake with some sweet tea sounds good."

Kaycee's brow raised. "It will be good after you eat your salad."

Sidra was such a junk-food junkie, and Kaycee wanted her to change her habits now that she was eating for two. It had been three weeks since she'd told Kaycee of her condition.

Since then, however, Kaycee had been so wrapped up in being with Kendrick that she hadn't had a chance to talk to her friend to find out if she'd told Hampton that he was going to be a daddy.

She put in an order for two Asian sesame chicken salads and a small basket of whole-grain baguettes before joining Sidra in the dining area.

"So what's been happening with you, girl-friend?" Kaycee asked sitting across from her friend. "Are you feeling good? Because you are sure looking good."

Sidra, attractive before, was now outright glowing as a result of the pregnancy. Her hair appeared to be shinier and her eyes brighter.

Sidra blushed. "I'm doing well, considering."

"So, have you told Hampton about the baby yet?"

She nodded. "Yep."

"And? What did he say?"

Sidra smiled half-heartedly. "He said he wasn't trying to be a daddy, especially to the child of some ho that he had a one-night stand with."

Kaycee's face fell and she seized her friend's hand in an effort to comfort her. "I'm sorry."

A lone tear rolled down Sidra's cheek, and she quickly wiped it away as she fought to keep from crying. "It's okay. It let me know what kind of person I was dealing with. Hampton Barnes is a jerk!"

"Sid, I'm sorry. I really am."

"It's my own fault. I am a sucker for fine men with money." She laughed.

"Don't worry, we will get through this together. You have my support all the way."

Sidra smiled. "Thanks, girlfriend, I'm going to need all the help I can get." She patted her flat stomach. "I know that I'm still in my first trimester, but this baby is already kicking my butt. I get so tired."

Kaycee laughed as she heard Sidra's tales of her pregnancy. By then, their food arrived and they dug in.

"So, how are things going between you and your man?" Sidra asked out the blue.

Kaycee's fork stopped en route to her mouth. She hadn't had the chance to talk to Sidra about how things had developed between her and Kendrick.

"Don't act like you don't know what I'm talking about," Sidra said. "I know you're seeing him."

"And if I was?"

Sidra shrugged. "I guess it would be your business."

Kaycee proceeded to fill Sidra in on the details of their relationship up until the present time.

"I knew you were going to be with him when you went on that fishing trip with him."

"How so?"

"Because you were focused on nothing else but being there with him. I envied that. When you turned down Grant I knew that you were already in love."

"I am," Kaycee confessed.

"That's cool," Sidra said. "My motto now is do what makes you happy. Since Kendrick's been in the picture I don't think I've seen you happier. I'm excited for you, Kaycee."

"Thanks, girl."

"Are you two talking marriage yet?"

"Not yet, but I have a feeling that it's going to happen."

She remembered Kendrick's question about her relationship with Paul ruining her belief in relationships.

"Does he want any children?"

Kaycee shrugged. "Actually, we haven't discussed that yet."

"Have you done it yet?"

"Sidra!"

"What?" Sidra groaned. "You know me. Sex is always on my brain."

"That's your problem."

"I know, literally, right?"

Kaycee reached for Sidra's hand. "I didn't mean it like that."

Sidra waved off Kaycee's comment with an airy gesture. "It's okay, it's the truth. But anyway, you were talking about the sex."

"No, you were," Kaycee shot back.

Sidra's brow raised. "You're not telling, are you?"

Kaycee sank back against the comfortable booth and looked to the ceiling. "All I can say is— whew!" She began fanning herself. While Sidra might have thought it was an action for the moment in their conversation, Kaycee really had to fan the flames.

"Better than Paul?"

All Kaycee did was roll her eyes in response. She and Paul had not been the most compatible in the bedroom. Where she was adventurous, Paul was conventional. Kaycee had resolved to conform to his style if they got married and the thought had unnerved her.

"Sounds like you got the whole package. Just make sure that he accepts you all the way. You don't want to be where I am. If I could turn back the hand, I would."

Sidra's words reverberated in Kaycee's mind long after she left. She needed somehow to get Kendrick's perspective on their life together.

Chapter 23

Telling the staff at Jireh came sooner than they had planned. Kendrick had totally forgotten about their hope to play it low-key when he arrived at work following his meeting.

Kaycee was helping Jaylen to bus tables while she talked to a guest and hadn't noticed him enter the building. Upon seeing her, he forgot everything.

As she made her way to the front, she spotted him and a warm smile lit up her face. All he could see was the love glowing on her face.

Without thinking, he sauntered right over and

hugged her up tight and kissed her. It was like something out of an old Western movie.

La Jetta, who was standing behind the front counter, popped her eyes open in surprise. At first, Kaycee tensed up, but it wasn't long before she gave in and wrapped her arms around his neck, receiving him completely.

Diners in the area began to clap and howl, bringing the rest of the staff from the back. Realizing that they had let the cat out of the bag, Kendrick released Kaycee, allowing her to slide down the length of his body.

"I guess our secret is out now," she said with a smile, hiding her blushing face in the crook of his neck.

"I'm sorry, I know we said we wouldn't, but I wasn't thinking about anyone or anything except being closer to you," he murmured against her ear.

The staff surrounded them with questions.

"It's about time!" Otis barked. "I could have told you there was something between them."

"Oh, shut up, old man!" Charlotte hollered. "You wouldn't know love if it came up and bit you on the butt!"

Everyone laughed.

"Is that right?" he asked with a wicked grin and shook his head. "Remember those words."

Kaycee noticed Charlotte pause before shooing him off with a wave of her hand.

The story of Kendrick and Kaycee's newfound love was repeated throughout the day to customers and second-shift staff members who had not been fortunate enough to have witnessed it firsthand.

Later, after they closed down, Kaycee decided to leave her car parked and ride home with Kendrick. Kaycee was grateful that he was driving his pickup truck with the bench seat, which meant that she could snuggle against him as they drove home.

Kendrick turned on the jazz station. Kaycee couldn't think of a better way to end the evening than to be listening to some soothing music while wrapped in her lover's arms on their way home.

That night they decided to stay at his house. He pressed the garage-door opener and parked the truck beside his Jeep.

Like a gentleman, he got out and walked around, opening Kaycee's door. Arm in arm, they entered the house. Once inside, he turned on the television in the family room then went into the kitchen to find something to drink.

Kaycee slipped out of her shoes and curled up on the sofa underneath a chenille throw.

Kendrick returned with two glasses of champagne with strawberries floating it. He handed one to Kaycee.

"Hmm, what's this?" she asked, taking a sip.

"Just relax," he replied, sitting down beside her. He pulled her against his chest and sighed thoughtfully.

"I wish it could be like this all of the time," Kaycee said, as if reading his mind.

"It can be."

She turned to look up at him with question in her eyes.

"How?" she dared to ask.

"We can move in together," he replied.

Kendrick's words were not what Kaycee wanted to hear and she moved away from him. She was seeking something more permanent. Kendrick's words made the joy and contentment that she had been feeling moments earlier dissolve.

"You don't want to live together?" he asked.

She shook her head in confirmation. "I can't do that. Moving in with you would be like taking steps backwards."

"Did you live with Paul?"

"No we did not, thank goodness," she exhaled with relief. Their breakup would have been much worse if that had been the case. "He was too conservative for that."

"What are you?" he challenged.

She stood from her spot on the couch and paced the floor. How could she tell him what she was truly thinking without starting an argument? However, she could not and would not compromise her beliefs for a man again. She'd done that once before and had ended up wasting years of her life.

"Kendrick, I love you, but I can't live with you. I have too much respect for myself to live with a man without a commitment."

Kendrick stood up beside her. "So you don't think we are committed?"

"Not in the way that it should be if we were to live together."

"And how is that?" he asked.

"Well, I think that when a man and woman come together to make a home, they should be joined in a committed legal relationship like marriage."

He walked closer to her. "So, you're telling me that you think the only way a man and woman should live together is if they are married?"

Kaycee bit her bottom lip nervously. The man standing before her was everything she wanted, and her words could possibly end the soul connection that they shared. The thought frightened her, bringing her close to tears. She closed her eyes, preparing herself for whatever he had to say, and nodded. When she opened her eyes, Kendrick was kneeling on the floor before her.

"I feel the same way, too." He held up an emerald-cut, icy-white diamond in a platinum setting. "Kaycee Jordan, will you make me the happiest man on earth and be my wife?"

Her eyes widened and her mouth dropped open. Her breathing speeded up as tears surfaced in her eyes. One after the other, they began to roll down her cheeks.

Kendrick took Kaycee's left hand and slipped the ring on her finger.

"So, what do you say?" he asked.

"Oh, my God!" she cried. "Are you for real?"

"Very."

She began to sob.

Kendrick pulled her down on his lap and kissed away her tears. "Kaycee, I know it's only been a few months, but it seems like years. At first, when Amanda passed, I couldn't see being married again, sharing my intimate thoughts with another woman.

"But, when I met you, I knew God was giving me a second chance at love, and none of the obstacles— our age difference, work relationship—made me change my mind.

"We are so good together. You are the missing piece to my puzzle. I can't see my life without you in it."

Kaycee's head fell forward against his shoulder and she wept for joy.

"Hey," he lifted her chin with his forefinger, "are you going to tell me yes or what?"

Through tear-streaked eyes she nodded emphatically. "Yes! Yes! Yes! Yes!"

She put all of her weight against him and they stumbled to the floor where she proceeded to confirm her response.

Chapter 24

Kendrick thought he was going to pass out. Either that or rip off their clothes and make love to Kaycee right there in the vestibule. He took a step back, surprised and very pleased at the vision before him.

Kaycee looked as delicious as the candy she was known for making. The dress she wore looked as though it had been designed especially for her luscious body. The neckline of the dark-chocolate garment dipped enough to show the right amount of cleavage accentuated by a simple yet elegant diamond necklace. It stopped at the knee, displaying her smooth legs, which he could imagine wrapped around his waist.

He gazed back up to her face; she had fashioned her hair into a sexy, layered Mohawk style and her gorgeous eyes made him weak every time he looked deeply into them.

"Are you just going to stand there or do I get a kiss?" she asked with her hands on her hips.

"You ain't said nothing but a word!" he exclaimed, giving her a big, hearty squeeze. Their mouths connected with tenacious hunger. For a hot second, he thought about skipping the whole evening event and going straight upstairs to his bedroom where they could make love again. The thought brought forth all sorts of positions that he had on reserve.

Kaycee interrupted his fantasizing with a tap on his shoulder. "Kendrick, if we keep it up like this we will never be able to go anywhere."

"I can't help that you're so fine," he teased, with a pat on her rear.

She smiled. "Thank you, but I'm excited about this evening. I'm looking forward to finally meeting some of your friends."

He released his hold with a shrug. "I would call them associates more than anything, but nevertheless, it is an honor to escort such a fine, sexy woman."

"No, it's an honor to be with such a distinguished and handsome man," she retorted, slipping her arm through his.

Kendrick glanced down at her hand and the brilliant ring on her finger. It made him both excited and proud that soon they would be husband and wife. Once they had become physically involved, Kendrick had been more determined than ever to make an honest woman out of her. She was a real lady and he didn't want to make light of that by suggesting that she compromise her principles to be with him. The pair decided a two-month engagement was long enough. Both preferred an intimate ceremony with family and close friends. Kaycee had already begun to pore over wedding magazines for gowns. They wanted their day to be very special.

After gathering her purse and the keys to his Jeep, the couple exited the house with nothing more than a promising outlook on their new lives.

The pier on the lake was filled with people loading into the large cruise boat. Warm yellow lights were strung along the deck, casting a seductive glow.

From the minute they entered the vehicle, Kendrick and Kaycee could not keep their hands off each other. It started with Kendrick rubbing on Kaycee's knee and continued with her distracting him as he drove, by caressing and stroking him in between stolen kisses.

Kendrick was grateful that they had made it to their destination without causing an accident.

"You are a bad girl!" he told her with a swat on the butt as they exited the Jeep.

Kaycee just laughed, enjoying the sensual teasing of the evening and looking forward to the promise of similar pleasure later in the night.

Kaycee was so drunk from their escapades that she didn't pay attention to any of the signage welcoming the partygoers aboard. All she could see was Kendrick leaning above her, with the look of love in his eyes.

They continued tickling each other here, tapping there, like mischievous little children, as they boarded the vessel and stopped at the table where Kendrick handed over his tickets.

It wasn't until they went inside the ballroom located in the middle of the boat that Kaycee really took in the atmosphere. Although on a smaller scale, the boat's opulence was reminiscent of the Titanic, with ornate light fixtures and rich brass railings and trim.

"Baby, this is nice," she said in awe.

Before he could reply, Kendrick felt a firm hand on his shoulder and turned around to find two of his high-school buddies.

"If it ain't Mr. Football!" one of the men joked.

"Ronald Pierre!" Kendrick shouted and gave the man a brotherly hug.

"What's up, K?" chuckled the other man, who looked to be about as tall as he was round.

"Is that you, Shrimpy?" Kendrick asked. He couldn't believe that the man standing before him weighed about a buck fifty in high school when he'd played kicker on their football team.

"I can't believe you made it after all these years!" Ronald exclaimed. "I thought you made Cali your home."

"I did," Kendrick replied. "But I came back to be closer to my daughter."

Ronald and Shrimpy's eyes fell on Kaycee.

"Look at you with a daughter," Ronald began. "Baby girl, your daddy was a trip back in the day."

Kendrick's eyes widened at Ronald's mistake. He was about to say something when Kaycee sweetly corrected him. "I'm sure my daddy *was* a trip back in his day, but let's not talk about him. I would rather hear the dirt on my fiancé, here," she said, stroking the lapel of Kendrick's suit jacket. She pretended to dust it off before standing on her tiptoes to plant a kiss on his mouth.

Ronald and Shrimpy's eyes bucked. Ronald peered at Kendrick for confirmation, and he nodded, amused at the looks on their faces.

Pulling Kaycee within his embrace, Kendrick proceeded to introduce them.

"Fellas, meet my fiancée, Kaycee Jordan. Kaycee, this is Ronald Pierre and Doug Waters, aka Shrimpy."

"Nice to meet you, boys," Kaycee said sweetly.

"I don't mean to sound too forward but—hot damn!" Ronald shouted.

Laughing, he and Shrimpy gave each other high fives.

"Seriously, you got any friends?" Ronald asked.

Sidra immediately came to mind, but went out just as fast. Her soon-to-be-mommy friend would have a fit if she brought Ronald home as a prospect.

"Sorry," she replied sweetly.

"So, who's all here?" Kendrick asked, looking around.

"Folks you probably don't remember and if you do, you don't want to see," Shrimpy said, taking a sip of his drink.

"So, Shrimp, where's Loretta?" Kendrick asked. Last he'd heard, Shrimpy and his common-law wife had finally got married after fifteen years of shacking up.

Shrimpy replied with a throat-cutting motion, indicating that they were through.

Kendrick laughed. "I thought you two had finally got it together."

"I did, too," Shrimpy answered. "But apparently, she was getting it together with the cable man, as well, because she upped and left with him out of the blue."

"I keep telling him it was the free cable!" Ronald joked.

The group laughed. At that moment three women approached. One could tell that they had been beautiful, but fast living had aged them beyond their forty-eight years. Even so, they seemed dead set on maintaining looks that did nothing to compliment them.

The one in the tight red dress stepped forward. The clinginess of the material revealed she wasn't wearing a girdle, judging by the bulge protruding around her waist. She wore long micro braids that draped over one shoulder.

She looked around at the group and smiled. "Hey fellas, when did you all get in?"

"Sonji Nelson," Ronald greeted, looking her over from head to toe. When she turned away he shuddered in disgust.

"Hey, Ronnie, Shrimp," she replied with a nod then looked over at Kendrick with a gap-toothed smile. "Hey, Kenny."

"Sonji."

Sonji was the girl all the football players had gone to for a good time and she had obliged them. She didn't care as long as it meant she could be associated with them. After all these years, it appeared she hadn't changed.

"So, who we got here?" Sonji asked, noticing Kaycee standing there for the first time.

"Hi, I'm Kaycee Jordan," Kaycee introduced herself with confidence.

"Kaycee is Kendrick's fiancée," Ronald announced, giving Shrimpy a high five again.

The women collectively gasped.

Sonji studied Kaycee for a few seconds. "Did you say your name is Kaycee Jordan?"

Kaycee nodded.

Sonji shook her head with a slow smile. "Well, I'll be. It is a pleasure to meet you, Kaycee Jordan," she said, singing her name.

Kaycee didn't understand where Sonji's strange behavior was coming from, but she returned the salutation. The three women walked a short distance before Sonji stopped them and started talking. All three turned to look at the pair and took off cackling like a group of hens.

"What was that all about?" Kaycee asked, perturbed.

"Don't worry about them," Kendrick replied. "Let's go get something to drink."

Kendrick announced that he would meet with the men later in the evening as they departed for the bar.

As they walked along, Kaycee leaned into his sturdy torso. She wanted more than anything to feel comfortable in his setting. She knew people would have suspicions about her age, but to actually verbalize them was something different. It lacked the tact and class that she was accustomed to. Now she knew why Kendrick referred to them as associates.

Kaycee knew she could use a drink. When they stopped at the bar, Kendrick ordered a white wine for her and a beer for himself.

They sat on the stools before the bar and he pulled

her toward him and began to rub her back sooth-
ingly. He was grateful that Kaycee's back was to the
crowd because he could see that they were the topic
of conversation.

When stares came his way, he boldly returned
them, which quickly caused them to be averted. The
only reason he regretted attending this event was his
desire to protect Kaycee's feelings.

By the time they'd had a second drink, Kendrick
was ready to go. He reached over and smoothed
Kaycee's bangs.

"This scene is boring me. Are you ready to go?"

"Actually, it's been fun being the center of attention."

His mouth dropped open in surprise. "You—you
recognized that?"

She turned to him and smiled. "Kendrick, I know
hateration when I see it."

She gazed around the room without looking at
anyone in particular. "Which is why I think we
should give them a reason to flap their gums."

She stood up and wiggled her hips between his
knees. Wrapping her arms around his neck, she
boldly claimed his mouth with her tongue. Kendrick
was thrown off by her outright behavior, yet turned
on all the same, and he pulled her tightly to him.

Thoughts ran through his head. Everybody would

have to recognize that she was his choice and that she was his, and no one else's opinion mattered.

At least, that's what he thought.

"Kaycee Janae Jordan, what in the world are you doing!"

Kaycee turned around to find a fuming Russell and Katherine Jordan.

Chapter 25

Kaycee's face contorted with confusion. "Mama, Daddy, what are you doing here?" she asked, dropping her arms at her sides.

"The question is what are *you* doing here?" her mother asked sharply.

"I thought you had a reunion to go to."

"This *is* the reunion!" her mother hissed with exasperation.

The blood drained from Kaycee's face, and she squeaked softly. "*This* is?"

Russell stepped forward, his arms crossed before

his chest authoritatively. "You better do some ex-
plaining and you better do it fast!" he barked.

Kaycee flinched at the harsh tone he used. She had
never known her father to talk to her in such a way.
As a result of their loud voices, people began to
crowd around them, causing Kaycee to grow hot
with embarrassment.

"I came with my fiancé, Kendrick," Kaycee announced.

"Your what!" Russell and Katherine shrieked in
unison.

Kaycee held up her hand to display her engagement ring. "We got engaged the other night. I'm
sorry I didn't tell you before, but I was planning to
surprise you both with it this weekend."

Kaycee glanced up at Kendrick's face and noticed
his blank expression. She took both of his hands in
hers and squeezed them with assurance. Despite the
fact that they were just now learning about the man
she adored, she knew that they would love him just
the same. She stepped forward.

"Mommy, Daddy, this is—"

"Get away from my daughter, Kendrick!" Russell
warned through gritted teeth.

Kaycee's eyes widened in surprise. A gnawing
feeling crept into her stomach and her mind twisted
with angst. This meeting wasn't turning out the way
she'd hoped.

Kendrick stepped away from Kaycee. "Russell, I know this is hard for you, but—"

"Negro, you don't know *what* it is to me!" her father yelled, rushing Kendrick. "I ought to kick your—"

Before he could get his hands on Kendrick, several of the men around them jumped and grabbed Russell. Shrimpy and Ronald held on to Kendrick.

"Russell, I know you're angry—"

"You don't know how I'm feeling!" Russell charged at Kendrick a second time.

"Daddy, what are you doing?" Kaycee cried. She couldn't believe her eyes. The man she had always known to be calm and together had never acted out with such violence and she felt it was all her fault. Her eyes filled with tears.

"What am I doing?" he shouted incredulously. "I'm trying to protect your honor!"

"My honor!" Kaycee gasped. She didn't know if her father was trying to imply that her honor needed protection because she was in the family way, but he couldn't be further off course. "My honor doesn't need protection. Kendrick hasn't done anything to ruin my reputation."

Katherine shushed her and snatched her back by the arm.

"Baby girl, you stay out of this," her father huffed.

"Stay out of it? Stay out of what?" Kaycee screamed in frustration, wrangling herself out of her mother's grip. She hurried over to where Kendrick stood. "Are you upset about his age? Well, don't worry, we covered that. If we're both okay with it then you should be happy for us."

"Kay, it's more than that," Katherine spoke up.

Kaycee searched her mother's face for answers. She looked at Kendrick, standing with his head hanging. "More? What is it?"

Kendrick took Kaycee's face in his hands. "Baby, you're going to have to listen to me before you take all this in."

"Let her alone, Thompson!" Russell started up again and the men began to pull him off the scene to calm him down. He bucked to free himself, but was unsuccessful.

Kendrick ignored him. "Kaycee, you know how we talked about our past and how we wanted to bring everything forth so that there would be no misunderstandings?"

Kaycee nodded. "Go on."

"Well, there was one thing I did not mention."

"What's that?" she asked, trying to focus her attention on something to block out her the harsh words her father was shouting, but his words came through loud and clear.

"He killed your Aunt Vickie!"

The whole room collectively gasped from surprise.

"Tell her, Thompson, how you killed my sister!"

The men quickly herded Russell out of the room, and her mother followed. Kendrick pulled a disoriented Kaycee away from the crowd and onto the deck.

Kaycee had never met her aunt because she had died before Kaycee was born, but from what she could remember she'd been killed in an automobile accident, not at some man's hands.

She turned back to Kendrick for confirmation. "What is he talking about?"

Kendrick was looking at the floor, his position revealing that her father's claims were probably true.

He began to explain as if in a trance.

"Back in college, I used to mess around with Vickie. She was a freshman when I was a senior being looked at by NFL teams. I was young and wasn't thinking about being serious, all I was thinking about was playing ball. After a while, Vickie and I kind of fell off. It was about two months later when I was in Alabama at a game that my roommate called saying that Vickie came to our place acting weird. He said she was crying and babbling and wasn't making sense."

"What was wrong with her?" Kaycee asked.

"He didn't know, but he said I needed to call her. So I called her. She sounded real messed-up on the phone, like she was drunk or something. I asked her what was wrong and she said she was in love with me and didn't want to live if we couldn't get married. I asked her why did she want to get married being that we broke things off, but she was insistent. I told her I couldn't and had to get off the phone and she told me that she was coming to Alabama to talk."

He paused, a weariness covering him like a blanket as he related the final details of his story. His eyes slowly closed and his head fell into his hands.

"I thought she was bluffing. I didn't think she would try to come but she did. About an hour across the Alabama state line, she...she lost control of her car, crossed the median and ran head-on into a tractor trailer. She died instantly."

Kaycee didn't know if she should hug him or not. After all, the woman he was talking about was her aunt, her flesh and blood. All her life, she'd heard great things about her Aunt Vickie. She was told that she shared her aunt's enthusiasm for life and her stubborn streak. Her father had obviously been protective of his baby sister. Their relationship was often compared to hers and Kyle's. She knew that her aunt's death had hurt her father deeply. Seeing him so full of rage and out of control for the first time ever was a testament to that fact. She'd always wondered about the woman she'd never known. Hearing that her only love and soul mate was somehow connected to her aunt's death was hard to swallow.

"Kendrick, I don't know what to say."

His head shot up, revealing tears and he gripped her by the forearms.

"Baby, please let's work through this."

Kaycee held her hands up and took a few hesitant steps backward. "I don't know."

He pulled her close to him. "Don't make a decision about us based on this, baby," he pleaded. "You know we belong together. We can get counseling to deal with this."

"She was my family, Kendrick," Kaycee replied, shaking her head.

"I know, I know," he whispered. Clasping his hands together, he lowered himself before her. "Please don't give up on us because of this. Let's work through it. Please, Kaycee. Please—"

"Kaycee, it's time to go."

The commanding sound of her mother's voice cut through their discussion.

Kaycee looked up at her mother and then back at Kendrick, submissive before her. Katherine looked at Kendrick and shook her head in pity.

"Let's go," she said. "We need to get your father back to the hotel."

Kaycee nodded. She turned to Kendrick and touched his shoulder before announcing that she was leaving. Kendrick remained in his position, hoping and praying that she wasn't going to walk away. After a few minutes, he looked up to find that she was gone.

* * *

His ride home was silent. Kendrick could not believe that he had held Kaycee in his arms and lost her in the same day.

The last people he'd expected to see were her parents. It had never dawned on him that Kaycee was related to the woman to whom he caused so much pain, and he realized the awkward position that her parents were in.

When he turned his truck into their subdivision, he felt like an empty man. Kaycee was supposed to be with him. They were supposed to decide whose house they were going to stay at for the night. He was supposed to make good on his promise to make love to her, slow and sweet. The ache in his body matched the ache in his heart as he turned onto their street.

Kaycee's house was dark. He stopped the truck beside her mail box and stared at the structure, as if trying to will her to walk out of the front door and into his truck, but he knew it would not happen. Kaycee was probably somewhere with her parents.

It made him cringe to think about all of the things they could be saying to fill her head and turn her against him. He closed his eyes and prayed that the Lord would give him wisdom and peace.

Chapter 26

The hours turned into days without a word from Kaycee. Kendrick realized that she needed time to process everything, but he trusted that their love would have her call him back into her life, but she didn't.

The fact that she might be gone broke his heart. Kendrick pulled the staff together and broke the news. Everyone rallied around him in support and took up the slack caused by Kaycee's absence.

Day in and day out, Kendrick didn't know if he was coming or going. He left home early in the day to come back late into the night without time to do anything but sleep. When he was feeling particularly sentimental he slept in his office, refusing to be around anything that reminded him of his beautiful brown-skinned, brown-eyed beauty.

On one particular evening he was stretched out in his recliner watching the sports channel, and he thought of the last time he and Kaycee had been together watching television and cheering on the team du jour. They'd had so much fun laughing, hollering at referees or players when they made bad calls or plays and recreating plays. He also remembered soft tackling her on the sofa where he proceeded to make a touchdown of his own.

He smiled as he remembered her gasping and then exhaling with satisfaction as he brought her completely under his submission with a stroke of his tongue against her sensitive and intimate places. When her body quivered uncontrollably in release, he mounted her with the urgency of all the stored love and passion that he felt for her. Later as he wrapped her body up against him, he professed his love to her over and over like a mantra until he fell asleep with Kaycee fulfilling his fantasies in his dreams.

Reality sank in quickly, bringing him back to the present, where he sat in his home all alone. Kaycee was gone. All they shared was gone. A pang of disappointment hit his heart. He turned off the television and closed his eyes, allowing the mourning process to begin.

* * *

"Where are you going?" Katherine Jordan asked her daughter as she entered the guest room and saw that Kaycee was packing. It had been almost two weeks since the fiasco at the reunion and she had grown accustomed to having her daughter home again in their protective custody.

"Mom, I do have my own place you know," Kaycee gently reminded her.

"I know, but do you have to go now? Your father was about to fire up the grill."

"Then you need to fire it up without me. I'm going home to get some things. I have to be at the airport in two hours."

Thank God for perfect timing. She was on her way to Detroit to be with her best cousin Alexa. She and her husband Darius were expecting their first baby, and she had promised to be there for the birth.

Besides, they needed to talk. Since they were kids, Kaycee had always admired her older cousin. Alexa was not only beautiful, but she was also very smart and knew what she wanted in life. While these were admirable characteristics, Alexa would be the first to say that they also became her downfall. However, she was able to overcome herself, reunite with her first love and start up a ministry helping women realize their purpose in life.

Alexa and Darius's testimony on how they had to

fight through many devils to be together touched Kaycee's life and she needed to be in the company of someone who had walked in her shoes and who could give her good advice. So she'd called Alexa, who was more than happy to have her come.

"Kaycee, do you think it's a good idea to go home?"

Kaycee whirled around with irritation. "Yes, it's a good idea. If you're worried about me seeing Kendrick, don't. I'm capable of handling myself."

"I just don't want to see you hurt again," her mother calmly replied.

Kaycee immediately felt bad for snapping off. She walked across the room to give her mother a hug. "You're right, Ma. I'm sorry for yelling. You just don't understand."

Katherine took Kaycee's hand and led her over to the sofa.

"Try me."

Kaycee was thrown off by her mother's attempt at objectivity concerning her relationship with Kendrick, but she looked at it as a window of opportunity to bare her soul and perhaps build an alliance in the process.

"Ma, Kendrick is really a very nice man. He cares for me and about me. He's never disrespected me. I never questioned his love for me."

"But he lied."

"He didn't lie," Kaycee challenged. "He had no

reason to tell me about that. He didn't even know we are related."

"Kayce, I know Kendrick Thompson. As far back as I can remember he's always been this pretty-boy playboy. He's the kind of man who's used to women approaching him and doing all of the work in a relationship, and then he walks away when he gets bored or tired. Look what happened to Vickie."

"Well, the Kendrick I know is not any of those things. Since we've met, he's been nothing but kind, loving and thoughtful."

Katherine groaned. "But why him, baby? He's old enough to be your daddy. You need to be with a man who is your age so you can grow together and someday have children."

"Mom, can't you see? I don't want any other man. Kendrick and I have this connection. We share the same goals, we both have the same likes and dislikes. I never thought I would find a man who loved James Bond or eating popcorn with M&Ms as much as I do.

"In the beginning, we thought about our age gap and the possibility of having a family. We tried to keep our relationship on the professional level, but we couldn't fight our feelings.

"You know how you can be with someone and not have to say any words, and when you do, sometimes you finish each other's sentences? Well, that's what it's like with Kendrick. Everything is so in sync. Right now, I think the most important thing is that we love each other." She reached over and grasped her mother's hands and looked her square in the eyes. "We really do. I know you know what I'm talking about because I've seen it in your relationship with daddy."

Katherine was quiet for a minute before softly replying, "I understand."

Kaycee exhaled with relief. "I have to try and talk to him, Mom."

"Like you said, you are an adult. I need more time to mull this over, maybe search my heart before I can give my blessing."

Kaycee gave her mother a big hug and kiss and ran off to finish packing.

It wasn't long before Kaycee was turning into her subdivision. She prayed that she wouldn't see Kendrick because she didn't know how she would respond to him. However, her prayers were thwarted when she approached her house and saw his car alongside another in his driveway.

She quickly pressed the button on the garage-door opener and drove inside, closing it before she could be seen. From there she went directly to her bedroom where she began to pack.

About an hour later, Kaycee descended the stairs, suitcase in hand. She placed it on the bottom step beside her carry-on bag and purse and went to the kitchen to straighten before she left.

As she stood at the kitchen window, she noticed movement in Kendrick's backyard. She leaned closer to the window to find him standing beside, of all people, Martinique Rivers!

The glass that she was holding fell from her hand and shattered into a hundred pieces. She cursed lightly and reached into the sink to pick up the shards while trying to figure out why Martinique was at her fiancé's house. A piece of glass grazed her finger, breaking the skin.

"Oh, my!" she exclaimed and quickly turned on the cold water. When it looked as if the blood had co-agulated enough to cut back on the bleeding, she wrapped her wound in a paper towel. She walked around to the dining room, which gave her a better view of Kendrick's backyard, but by this time the pair were gone.

She hurried to the library in the front of the house and peeked through the curtains just in time to see what she feared—Kendrick embracing Martinique. Kaycee couldn't believe her eyes. When he released his hold on her, he opened her car door, allowed her to get settled inside and shut it behind her. Leaning down, he said some final words before she pulled off. As he turned back to go inside, Kendrick paused long enough to look at her house.

Kaycee froze at her place in the window, wondering if she had been seen, but he made no acknowledgement and went inside.

She stepped away from the window, holding her stomach. She felt like throwing up. One week away from him and he brings another woman into the picture.

Quickly, she gathered her things and carried them out to her car. She didn't have time to ponder over what had taken place in the last week. She might go crazy. She just needed to get out of Atlanta.

Chapter 27

"Kaycee, I'm sorry," Alexa apologized for the umpteenth time since she'd arrived in Detroit.

The pair were in Alexa's car whizzing down the expressway back to her side of town in Southfield.

"Alex, it's okay," Kaycee assured her again.

"I forgot that I rescheduled this session because of the upcoming holiday. I couldn't disappoint them," she said, referring to the women's business support group that was a spin-off of her magazine.

"I'm surprised that you're still having sessions in your condition." She said referring to her cousin's expanded girth. Alexa was in her ninth month, due any day.

"Why not?" she asked matter-of-factly. "If I was on someone's job I would have to work up to the time to deliver. Besides, I enjoy what I do. The women are so great."

Kaycee was impressed by her cousin's recent success.

Since she and her husband had relocated to Detroit three years ago, Alexa had started up her own magazine, *Proverbs 31 Woman.* The magazine addressed areas of interest to the Christian woman, such as balancing marriage, family and career. She had firsthand experience in that arena. The magazine had been so well received that she'd started up incubator groups that helped women to identify their life purpose and how to make them into a reality in their lives.

As usual, Kaycee was very proud of the strides that her cousin had made in her personal and professional life. She hoped that she could glean from her the tools that she needed to work through her own issues.

About twenty minutes later, Alexa was parking her Volvo XC90 in the parking lot of a four-story office building. Kaycee jumped out first and ran around to help Alexa. Both laughed when Alexa had to put her seat back in order to get from behind the wheel.

"I know, I'm big as a house!" Alexa said with a giggle. "But my man likes it."

"That's all that matters," Kaycee said, laughing along with her.

They took the elevator up to the fourth floor to the headquarters of *Proverbs 31 Woman*. A young college-age-looking woman sitting behind the desk looked up to greet them.

"Your husband just called, Mrs. Riverside," she informed Alexa, handing her the half-written message.

"Thanks, Dani," she turned to Kaycee. "Dani works for me in the evenings. She's a student over at the university. Dani, this is my cousin, Kaycee Jordan."

The young girl stood and extended her hand. "Pleased to meet you."

"Likewise," Kaycee replied.

She glanced around the office at the purple-and-gold decor and smiled. "I really like the color scheme. It looks so regal."

Alexa nodded. "I knew you would get it." She turned back to Dani. "Let me know when the ladies arrive."

Alexa gave Kaycee a quick tour of the small office space before leading her back to her own office. She eased down onto a comfortable sofa with a groan. She closed her eyes and fanned herself with her hand.

"You okay?" Kaycee asked.

Alexa nodded. "I'm just ready to have the baby. I want my figure back."

"Knowing you, you will be back on point in no time at all. That is one of many great things I can say about you. You are so committed."

Alexa waved her comment off. "Little do you know that my only commitment throughout this pregnancy was to consistently put food in my mouth, but enough about me, what's going on with you? Did you get a chance to talk to Kendrick?"

Before Kaycee could reply, the intercom on Alexa's phone buzzed. It was Dani announcing the women's arrival. She gave Kaycee an apologetic look. "I'm sorry, Kayce."

"Girl, please. We have all night to talk."

With Kaycee's assistance, Alexa eased off the sofa and the pair went into what Alexa called the Creative Room. It was where the company held their staff meetings, but rather than do it around a large oval table, the room was outfitted with comfortable chairs and sofas.

The five women were already seated.

"Hello, ladies!" Alexa called out.

They each returned a greeting.

"I know this is our last meeting before the shuttle launches," she said, referring to her pregnancy. "As you know I'm due any day and my wonderful cousin Kaycee decided to come up from Atlanta to help out."

"How nice," one of the ladies commented.

"It is, isn't it?" Alexa agreed. "But anyway, I forgot that her plane came in today and we literally just got in from the airport, so I hope you don't mind if she joins us in session."

"Not at all," a woman named Cathy replied.

Alexa made a motion welcoming Kaycee to the group. When she was seated, she opened her notebook.

"The last time we met we were talking about how other's expectations can hinder us from our dreams and goals. Who wants to begin?"

A tall woman with a low, natural hairstyle raised her hand.

Alexa acknowledged her with a nod and said, "Since Kaycee doesn't know everybody and she is a guest, can you all state your names when you have the floor."

"Hi, Kaycee, I'm Diana. I'm trying to launch my first book and I'm having a problem because my family are not supportive of me. They depend on me to meet their needs, while setting mine to the side."

"How does that make you feel?" Alexa asked.

"Like I don't matter," Diana replied. "They know that since I was a small girl, I've been writing. God gave me the gift to write, but whenever I try to work on my book, they want me to set it aside to take care of their issues. They look at my writing as a hobby and not a career like I'm trying to make it into."

The women grunted and clicked their tongues in response.

Kaycee looked around at each of the women. She could easily be one of them. Had she not felt the same yearning to be a part of Café Jireh? She sat up in her chair to hear more.

A short woman sitting beside Kaycee raised her hand.

"Yes, Valerie," Alexa acknowledged her.

"I believe that God gives us all a desire for his purpose in our lives, but we have to recognize the strategies of the enemy to discourage us."

"Good point," Alexa replied. "So how can we—" she stopped when she saw Kaycee's hand shoot up in the air.

"Kaycee, you have a question?"

Kaycee nodded. "I'm sorry for interrupting, but I'm curious about the statement that Valerie made."

"Okay."

Kaycee hesitated as she searched for the right words. The whole idea that God would give every person a desire for something that was his purpose for them intrigued her.

"Well, does the desire that Valerie talked about pertain to jobs only? Can it apply to people, as well?"

"What do you mean?" Alexa asked.

"I mean, does God's purpose for our lives relate to careers or can it be a part of his plan for two people to come together?"

"I believe so," Cathy piped up. "I first met my

husband fifteen years ago when I was twenty-five. He was so determined to be with me, but I kept putting him off because I felt like he was stalking me. Despite this, he stayed near me and didn't give up. When I finally came to the Lord, it was revealed to me also that he was supposed to be my husband. We were married five years ago."

A woman who had been sitting quietly in the back listening stood up. "Kaycee, my name is Gayla and I'm fairly new to the group. One thing I've observed since I've been here is that no one speaks in code. We are all upfront about our issues because we want real resolution."

A host of "amens" filled the air.

Kaycee swallowed and looked at Alexa for support. Alexa gave her the nod. With a deep breath, Kaycee proceeded to tell the story of how she and Kendrick's lives had become entwined.

She talked about the immediate connection, the interests, companionship. She mentioned how he overcame his grieving-widower role and the objections of his grown daughter to be with her. With tears in her eyes and twirling the ring on her left finger, she told them how he'd asked her to be his wife.

Then she fast-forwarded the story to the scene at Kendrick's reunion, her parents' disappointed faces, her father's raging temper, and the true story about tragically losing her aunt. The conclusion involved her spying Martinique leaving the house. When she was finished there wasn't a dry eye in the house.

Cathy found the box of tissues and passed it around.

Kaycee took a tissue and wiped her eyes. "I'm sorry," she sobbed. "I didn't mean to take over your meeting like this."

"It's okay," Carla assured her, rubbing her back. "That's why we are here."

"That's right, Kaycee," Alexa added. "There's no set pattern to our meetings. I just introduce a topic and we free-talk, but in the end we all have to come up with viable solutions to our problems so that we can move forward."

"I wanted to talk to him, but I didn't know what to say. What do you say to a man after you find out something like this? My dad is crushed. It's like his sister died all over again. Then seeing that—that *thang* over at his house made me so angry."

"Kaycee, I know this may be hard, but you have got to pray and ask God if he is the one," Valerie said.

"If you ask me, I think he is," Diana retorted.

"But what about Ms. Thang!" Carla replied. "Is she supposed to pretend like that didn't happen?"

Gayla moved in closer to Kaycee. "Kaycee, Alexa is always telling us that when we handle adversity the first rule is to realize it's not about you and then jump to conclusions. That woman's visit could be totally innocent, you don't know until you ask."

"That's right, girl," Diana added.

Cathy got out of her seat and sat down on the sofa beside Kaycee. "Kaycee, remember how I said it was with my husband and me in the beginning? The signs were there, I just wasn't ready to accept them. You need to ask yourself if you're ready. Because if you are, nothing will stand in your way of believing the truth."

Kaycee slowly nodded her head as she wiped the remaining tears from her eyes. She was grateful to all of the ladies for helping her walk through her issue. She knew that it had been ordained for her to be there at that given moment.

"So, what are you going to do, girl?" Gayla asked.

"She's going to take me to the hospital," Alexa cut in.

All eyes turned on her. "My water broke."

Kendrick pushed the doorbell and waited. He looked around the Lincoln Street neighborhood in Savannah. The well-built Victorian homes were located in an older part of the city with stately oak trees lining the curbs. The neighborhood was on the mend with lots of the homes being rebuilt to their former glory because of their architectural, historical and cultural significance, thanks to concerned citizens.

The inner door opened and there stood Katherine.

"Can I help you?" she asked in a cold, distant voice.

"Hello, Katherine," he greeted.

"Can I help you?" she repeated.

"Katherine, is Russell home? I would like to talk to you both."

"Kendrick, what are you trying to prove coming to our home like this?" she hissed.

"Can we sit down and talk like adults?" he asked. "I wouldn't want your neighbors to have to be subjected to our conversation."

"What is there to say?" Katherine asked.

"Kat, who's at the door?" Russell called from the hallway.

Katherine opened the door wide enough so that Russell could see Kendrick standing there.

"Man, you have got a lot of nerve coming to my house!" Russell shouted, adjusting his pants. "You want me to finish what was started?"

"Russell, hear me out. I just need to talk to Kaycee."

"She's not here," Katherine replied.

"She's got to be here," he retorted. "I checked with her best friend Sidra and she said she hasn't heard from her in weeks."

"If she was here, do you think I'd let you see her?" Russell challenged.

"Russ, you may be her father, but I'm her fiancé and I know she would talk to me."

Russell grimaced. "Get the hell off my porch before I call the police!"

Kendrick stood there with a nonchalant look on

his face. His hands were buried in his pockets and he rocked back and forth as though he had nothing better to do.

"She's not here, Kendrick," Katherine announced again.

"Yes, she is." He leaned closer to the screen and called out. "Kaycee!"

"Kendrick, she's not here," she firmly repeated.

He ignored her comment. "Kaycee, come talk to me, please!"

Russell reached for the cordless phone and began to dial.

Kendrick pressed his hands against the locked screen door and shouted. "Kaycee, baby!"

Katherine shook her head. "Kendrick, she's not here, you may as well leave before it gets worse."

"I'm on the phone with the police!" Russell informed him. "If you don't leave my property now, Thompson, I'll tell them to send the boys."

Kendrick realized that he wasn't getting anywhere, and, not desiring to have anything mar his record, turned and walked away. He would have to get to Kaycee in another way.

The ambience in the labor and delivery room was peaceful with dim lighting and soft music playing. Kaycee glanced around the room and was grateful to see family who were there to offer support.

"You're doing good, baby!" Darius, Alexa's husband, encouraged as he wiped her brow with a cool damp cloth.

"One more push will do it, Alexa!" Dr. Robinson announced.

"You're doing good, Alex," Maya, her best friend, added from behind the video camera.

"Question is, do I look good?" Alexa joked, garnering laughter from everyone in the room.

"You look like a pro!" Maya replied with a thumbs-up.

"Baby girl, you are doing so good!" Alexa's mother Beverly said, rubbing her daughter's legs. "My grandbaby got a head full of hair!"

Kaycee stood by Alexa's feet where she had a good view of the baby's head sticking out. Never in a million years would she believe that a woman's vagina would stretch so wide. But that was another wonder of God.

She looked back at her cousin who was determined to get it over with, and quickly reassumed her job of holding Alexa's legs.

"Okay, everybody ready? Like I said, Alexa, one good long push will do it. Okay, one…two… three puuush!"

Alexa screamed as she bore down and pushed like she never had before. As she did, the baby slipped out into Dr. Robinson's waiting hands.

"Congratulations! It's a boy!"

Everyone screamed with joy. The doctor placed the wailing little boy on Alexa's chest. At the first glance of their baby, Alexa and Darius began to weep for joy.

"We did it, baby!" Darius cried.

"I know, thank you, Lord!" Alexa shouted. "Thank you, Father!"

Kaycee stood by while the doctor allowed Darius to cut the cord. The nurses quickly cleaned him up and swaddled him so that he could be placed back into his mother's waiting arms.

There were prayers and tears as baby Joshua Isaiah Riverside was passed around for all to admire. Everyone commented on how much he looked like his father with the exception of his mother's light brown eyes.

When it came Kaycee's turn to hold him, she was trembling like a leaf.

"Don't drop our baby, now," Darius teased.

"Don't worry," Kaycee replied, bringing him securely to her bosom. "I wouldn't dream of dropping this young prince."

She walked across the room, rocking him along the way while gazing at his handsome face and marveling at the size of his little nose and tiny hands.

"He's so beautiful," Kaycee whispered. At the sound of her voice, his little eyes blinked open. Right then and there, Kaycee felt the tug of motherhood pulling at her heartstrings. It was as if an angel had delivered a message. And she whispered a silent thank-you for answering her prayer.

Chapter 28

Café Jireh was eerily quiet. The usual patrons were there, the regular staff was in place, but it was missing something. Kendrick knew that the missing piece was Kaycee.

He sat in the dining room and peered out the window at the people passing by without really seeing them. Since the incident at the Jordan's home a week ago, he felt that he had exhausted all of his options. Kaycee wasn't answering her cell phone and her voice mail at home was full. Full of messages from him, no doubt.

With a sigh, he rested his bristly chin in his hand

and realized that he didn't remember the last time he'd shaved. He shook his head pathetically. Three weeks had passed and Kaycee was nowhere to be found. The realization that it might finally be over made him crazy.

"Kendrick," a voice called his name.

He looked up to find Martinique standing above him.

"How's it going, Martinique?"

"I should be asking you that!" she retorted in disdain. "Kenny, what is going on?"

He shrugged.

"We're planning your wedding. Why are you down in the dumps? Are you getting cold feet?"

He shook his head, dismissing that possibility. He didn't want her to get any ideas.

"Then what is it?" she asked, opening up her planner. "I've done everything that you asked me to do. I've paid the caterer and the band. I even got the white carriage on lock. What's going on?"

"I don't know if there's going to be a wedding."

"What!" Martinique exclaimed. "Tell me you're joking."

"I wish I was," he replied. Planning a wedding in Kaycee's absense and without her knowledge seemed like a good idea at first. He had hoped that everything would have smoothed over by then and wanted to get married right away. Now he wasn't sure it was a good idea after all.

"Why? What happened? Did she change her mind?"

"Did she change her mind," he repeated with a half laugh. "The question is, did she even know about it?"

Martinique couldn't believe her ears. She'd heard of people not having enough money for a wedding, or being real creative to have a one-of-a-kind event, but never had she planned a wedding without a bride in place.

"Kendrick, what are you doing?" she asked in exasperation. "Are you trying to waste my time or better yet your money? Does the child know that you want to marry her?"

He nodded. "I proposed, but a huge situation happened between me and her family."

The confused look on Martinique's face caused him to explain exactly what had transpired.

When he finished, she sank back against her seat in disbelief. "Oh, my goodness."

"Now, I don't know what to do. She's not answering her cell phone and I haven't seen life over at her house for weeks."

"Do you know where she is?"

He shook his head. "I have no idea."

"Then you need to go find her."

Kendrick gave Martinique a look that said "duh." He breathed deeply to control his annoyance.

"I've tried that," he reminded her, irritated by her thoughtless response.

Martinique grabbed his hand. "Kendrick, listen to me. You have got to get up, clean yourself up and go after her. I don't care what her parents say, you have got to give it all you've got and you can't stop. You got to make them understand that no matter what they say, she's going to be your wife."

Kendrick reared back at Martinique's take-charge approach. He found it surprising that she was championing the very woman whom she had considered competition a few months ago.

"It can't be that easy."

"Have you ever tried?" she asked, sipping her water. "What happened to the driven Kendrick Thompson that I knew?"

Kendrick shrugged. "I guess he got old."

"Whatever!" Martinique huffed. "He's in there and it's up to you to revive him. Pull out that Steeler spirit if you have to."

Kendrick smiled. "You think it will work?"

She nodded emphatically. "Hell, yeah. Besides, women like that kind of stuff. It lets us know you really care."

His expression softened. "Thanks, Martinique."

She shook her head. "No problem. I just need you to take care of your bride so that I can finish doing my job." She stood up and kissed him on the forehead. "I'm envious of Kaycee."

"Why?" he asked.

"Because she has a good man," she said and patted his shoulder.

"Thanks, Martinique," he called behind her.

As soon as she left, the first thing he did was get on the cell phone and call his barber. Martinique was right. He'd come this far and he wasn't about to let his future slip through his hands so easily.

The doorbell rang incessantly.

Kaycee, who was upstairs watching television, glanced at the clock on the nightstand and wondered who could be coming by at eight o'clock at night. She quickly dismissed it as one of her brothers coming by to see her parents and lay back down on the bed.

The bell rang again just as Katherine reached for the knob.

She was surprised to find Kendrick standing there again.

"What are you doing here?" she asked.

"I want my wife!" he told her firmly.

"She is not your wife," Katherine dryly replied.

"She will be," he replied. "May I come in?"

Katherine paused for a moment and realized she didn't want a repeat of his last visit with him yelling through the door, especially not at this hour.

Reluctantly, she undid the screen door and let him pass through.

"Thank you, Katherine," he said gratefully.

Katherine led him into the living room where he took a seat.

"Who's at the door, Kat?" Russell called from the family room in the back.

"I think you need to come out and see!" she replied.

The second Russell rounded the corner, his eyes narrowed in response. "What are you doing here?" he bellowed.

Kendrick stood up. "Wait, Russell, let's talk like men."

"I don't want to hear a damn thing you have to say!" Russell replied. "Now get out of my house."

"Russell, I've lived with the guilt of Vickie's death for years because I believed it was my fault. I wish I could take it all back, but I can't. I begged her not to come to Alabama, but you know how stubborn she was. She was determined."

"Why didn't you try to call us?"

"Russell, I was away in Alabama, the only way I could call her was by pay phone. If I'd known things would turn out that way, I would have called."

By now Kaycee had recognized Kendrick's voice and had rushed downstairs. Almost immediately, she could smell his presence. His aftershave was a pleasant memory. Her heart ached to hold him, but she knew that the conversation taking place had to be over before she could talk to him. She sat on the steps to listen.

"You killed my sister," Russell accused him. "First you hurt her then you killed her."

"Look man, I'm sorry that I got involved with her. I really am, but I can't change that. All I can do is do right by Kaycee."

"Over my dead body!"

"Russell!" Katherine shouted.

"Man, do you honestly believe that I would give my blessing to you after what happened?"

Kendrick nodded.

Russell laughed, smacking his knee. "Man, you are crazy."

"I am," Kendrick replied. "If crazy means coming this far for the woman I love, then I'm crazy."

"Kendrick, why Kaycee?" Katherine asked warily. "She's young enough to be your daughter. Why not marry a woman your own age?"

"Katherine, when my wife died seven years ago, I thought I was done with relationships. I didn't think my heart could love anyone on that level again, but then I met Kaycee. She's charming, beautiful and intelligent. We connected right away, like we'd known each other forever.

"I realized she was younger than me and believe me, I tried to keep my distance, but every day signs kept popping up telling me that we were supposed to be together."

"I don't want to hear this!" Russell boomed and turned his back.

"Please, hear me out," Kendrick pleaded.

Katherine nodded for him to continue.

"Kaycee is an exceptional woman. When she came to work with me at my restaurant, she came with a lot of fresh ideas that I wasn't even open to at first, but that is how she is. She can turn the heart of her greatest challenger and her love is pure. She doesn't try to push her opinions on others, she doesn't place stipulations on you, she just loves unconditionally and that's how she won my heart."

The room was quiet. When neither of the two responded, Kendrick took that as his cue to continue.

"I asked Kaycee to marry me because I love her. I would prefer that I have your blessing before we get married, but know that I don't intend to drag things out. She is a good woman and she deserves a proper wedding."

By this time the tears were flowing down Kaycee's face. He'd come for her, and he was willing to stand up against her parents to get their blessing. Her heart filled with joy.

Russell's shoulders heaved and tears fell down his face. Katherine gently rubbed his back.

"Kendrick, thank you for telling us how you feel

about our daughter. We already know how special she is and apparently she feels the same way about you. Knowing this, what kind of people would we be if we stood in the way of your love?"

He sighed with relief that the wall of resistance had come down. Clasping his hands in a prayerful gesture he lowered his head.

"Can you please, please tell me where I can find your daughter?"

"All you have to do is turn around," Katherine calmly replied.

Quickly, Kendrick did an about-face to find Kaycee standing there crying silently. Slowly he approached her and raised his hand to her face to wipe away her tears with his fingertip. Smoothing his palms down her arms he caught her hands in his own where he weaved his fingers through hers.

"I missed you," he whispered.

"I missed you, too."

He stood back and opened his arms, inviting her back into his world and she stepped into his strong embrace, knowing that she would never walk out again.

"I love you, Kaycee," he whispered to her, moving his lips against hers. "I won't stop, can't stop loving you."

Epilogue

The six-bedroom house was located on ten acres of land about an hour outside of the city. Kaycee and Kendrick fell in love with the sprawling property immediately. It was perfect. In addition to the house, there was a guest house out back, a barn and a corral that Kendrick planned to fill with cows, chickens and horses respectively.

It was truly a fairy tale come true for Kaycee. Who would believe that just two years ago, she was putting up with crap at Carrington Financial and now she would be shoveling it on her own property! However, she loved every bit of her new life.

From the master bedroom upstairs, she could see several cars lining the long driveway. The guests were arriving for the combined housewarming and homecoming taking place downstairs. She smiled back at her husband who was adjusting his clothes.

"Looks like everyone is here," she announced.

He walked up behind her, slipped his arms around her waist and began to nibble playfully on her neck.

"How much longer do we have?" he asked.

"Just another week," she informed him.

"I don't know if I can wait that long," he informed her.

"Truth be told, I'm not sure if I can, either," she replied, turning around to kiss him. Kendrick's hands skimmed up her hips and onto her full breasts when a soft knock on the door interrupted them.

"Yes!" Kaycee called out.

"Kaycee, everyone is here," her mother announced.

Hand in hand, the Thompsons exited their suite. Waiting in the hallway were Katherine and Russell with two bundles in their hands.

"Thanks, Mom, thanks, Dad," Kaycee said kissing them both as she took one and Kendrick the other. They exchanged hugs.

"Katherine, Russell, I'm very happy that you could make it," Kendrick announced, hugging them both.

It took awhile for Russell to come around, but he eventually did. He realized he wasn't right and asked

Kendrick to forgive him. Not only because it was the right thing to do but also because of Kaycee. It was important to him to restore their relationship. He was not only hurt about the situation with his sister, but he had to admit that he was afraid of losing his daughter to another man.

The four of them descended the stairs and went into the massive family room where all of their family and friends were located.

"Welcome to our new home!" Kaycee exclaimed. "And now for the grand finale."

At the same time, she and Kendrick removed the covering over the bundles they were holding to reveal two small babies.

"Everyone, say hi to our sons Kaydon Richard and Kuyler Russell."

Oohs and aahs filled the room, making Kaycee smile with joy. Bianca muscled her way to the front like a bratty four-year-old. Although she had seen the babies at the hospital when Kaycee gave birth, she was determined to see her baby brothers again.

"They look just like me!" she shouted over her shoulder.

Everyone laughed.

Kaycee knew the reality of her being Bianca's stepmother was hard for Kendrick's daughter to swallow, but the two had promised to take things day by day.

Kaycee looked up at Kendrick beaming with pride and joy. She beckoned for him to draw nearer and when he did, she kissed him sweetly.

"I love you so much!"

"I love you," he added.

For the first time since she had launched out to find herself, Kaycee felt she could say that she had finally found what she was looking for.

You can't hide from desire...

A GUILTY AFFAIR

National bestselling author

Maureen Smith

Journalist Riley Kane has long suspected that the death of
her fiancé—a San Antonio police officer—was not a simple
accident. So she reluctantly enlists the aid of his former
partner, Noah Roarke. But the sizzling desire surging
between Riley and Noah fills them each with incredible
longing...and unbelievable guilt.

Available the first week of May wherever books are sold.

He loved a challenge...and she danced
to the beat of a different drum.

Enchanting
MELODY

National bestselling author
ROBYN AMOS

Escaping poverty had driven Will Coleman to succeed on
Wall Street, but in his spare time he taught ballroom dancing.
Then into his dance studio walked Melody Rush, a feisty
society beauty who enjoyed the freedom of slumming.
And the enchanting dance of love began....

Available the first week of May wherever books are sold.

KIMANI
ROMANCE

www.kimanipress.com
KPRA0180507

A soul-stirring, compelling
journey of self-discovery...

journey
into My Brother's Soul

Maria D. Dowd

Bestselling author of
Journey to Empowerment

A memorable collection of essays, prose and poetry,
reflecting the varied experiences that men of color face
throughout life. Touching on every facet of living—love,
marriage, fatherhood, family—these candid personal
contributions explore the essence of what it means to
be a man today.

**"*Journey to Empowerment* will lead you on a
healing journey and will lead to a great love of self,
and a deeper understanding of the many roles we
all must play in life."—*Rawsistaz Reviewers***

Coming the first week of May
wherever books are sold.

www.kimanipress.com   KPMDD0290507

tangled
ROOTS

A Kendra Clayton Novel

ANGELA
HENRY

Nothing's going right these days for part-time
English teacher and reluctant sleuth Kendra Clayton.
Now her favorite student is the number one suspect in a local
murder. When he begs Kendra for help, she's soon on the road
to trouble again—trying to find the real killer, stepping into
danger...and getting tangled in the deadly roots of desire.

"This debut mystery features an exciting new
African-American heroine.... Highly recommended."
—*Library Journal* on *The Company You Keep*

*Available the first week of May
wherever books are sold.*

KIMANI PRESS™

www.kimanipress.com   KPAH0680507

Celebrating life every step of the way.

YOU ONLY GET *Better*

New York Times bestselling author

CONNIE BRISCOE

and

Essence bestselling authors

LOLITA FILES
ANITA BUNKLEY

Three fortysomething women discover that life, men and
everything else get better with age in this entertaining
three-in-one anthology from three award-winning authors!

Available the first week of March wherever books are sold.

KIMANI PRESS™
www.kimanipress.com

KPYOGB0590307